"She loves you, Cody."

It was dark, or he just couldn't see, but it felt like the very same thing, and Nina was curled up beside him like they hadn't lost seven years. Like those years didn't exist. Part of him didn't want them to.

But they did.

He wanted to believe there was some magic connection between father and child—so that he could believe Brianna had just loved him on sight, but that only meant there was something connecting him to Ace.

He didn't love his father. Maybe his feelings had been complicated as a child, but he'd never *loved* Ace.

"If she loves me, it's only because of you."

"I tried to give her everything I would have wanted her to have. I wanted her to have you, but I didn't think she could. So I did the best I could, but they were just stories."

"Stories that gave her a foundation of trust. We both know how hard trust is when you grow up in a dangerous situation, and you gave that to her."

COVERT COMPLICATION

NICOLE HELM

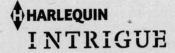

To my husband, the best dad I know.

ISBN-13: 978-1-335-13642-8

Recycling programs for this product may not exist in your area.

Covert Complication

Copyright © 2020 by Nicole Helm

This edition published by arrangement with Harlequin Books S.A.

For questions and comments about the quality of this book, please contact us at CustomerService@Harlequin.com.

Harlequin Enterprises ULC
22 Adelaide St. West, 40th Floor
Toronto, Ontario M5H 4E3, Canada
www.Harlequin.com

Printed in U.S.A.

Nicole Helm grew up with her nose in a book and the dream of one day becoming a writer. Luckily, after a few failed career choices, she gets to follow that dream—writing down-to-earth contemporary romance and romantic suspense. From farmers to cowboys, Midwest to *the* West, Nicole writes stories about people finding themselves and finding love in the process. She lives in Missouri with her husband and two sons and dreams of someday owning a barn.

Books by Nicole Helm

Harlequin Intrigue

A Badlands Cops Novel

South Dakota Showdown
Covert Complication

Carsons & Delaneys: Battle Tested

Wyoming Cowboy Marine
Wyoming Cowboy Sniper
Wyoming Cowboy Ranger
Wyoming Cowboy Bodyguard

Carsons & Delaneys

Wyoming Cowboy Justice
Wyoming Cowboy Protection
Wyoming Christmas Ransom

Stone Cold Texas Ranger
Stone Cold Undercover Agent
Stone Cold Christmas Ranger

Harlequin Superromance

A Farmers' Market Story

All I Have
All I Am
All I Want

Falling for the New Guy
Too Friendly to Date
Too Close to Resist

Visit the Author Profile page at Harlequin.com.

CAST OF CHARACTERS

Cody Wyatt—Youngest Wyatt brother, and a former undercover agent for a secretive group known as North Star. Dated Nina Oaks as a teenager.

Nina Oaks—Grew up on the neighboring ranch to Cody after being fostered. Broke up with Cody at a threat from his father, then found out she was pregnant and kept her daughter a secret from everyone.

Brianna Oaks-Wyatt—Cody and Nina's six-year-old daughter.

Ace Wyatt—Cody's father, who ran the Sons of the Badlands. He is currently in jail.

Grandma Pauline Reaves—Cody's grandmother raised him after his eldest brother got him out of the Sons.

Felicity Harrison—Nina's foster sister.

Brady Wyatt—Cody's brother; sheriff's deputy and EMT certified.

Gage Wyatt—Brady's twin; sheriff's deputy.

Tucker Wyatt—Cody's brother; detective.

Dev Wyatt—Cody's brother; lives and works at the Reaves ranch.

Chapter One

Moving back home to his grandmother's ranch was not what Cody Wyatt had envisioned for his adult life.

Despite being the youngest of six, despite having five bossy, obnoxious older brothers, Cody had never excelled at people telling him what to do. He accepted it from his grandmother—she'd raised him and his brothers, had *saved* him and his brothers. There was no challenging Grandma Pauline.

But he was pretty sure he was going to punch Dev's lights out if his brother kept criticizing the way he took off a horse's saddle.

It wouldn't be the first time he'd gotten in a physical fight with his brothers, but rarely did he get frustrated with Dev.

With six brothers, certain smaller relationships existed. The oldest, Jamison had saved all of them from their father's biker gang and secreted them out to Grandma—their late mother's mother. Jamison had tried to father him, and Cody had allowed it and chafed at it in turn. He looked up to his oldest brother, but there were so many years between them, and such a feeling of *responsibility* on Jamison's shoulders that Cody hadn't understood when they'd been younger.

Brady and Gage were twins, their own playmates and companions—operating on their own frequency. Cody loved them, respected them, but they were two sides of the same coin who spoke their own darn language half the time.

Tucker, closest in age to Cody, idolized Jamison. Tuck shared that core goodness about him that Jamison had, with a little less martyrdom weighing him down.

But Dev had shared that angry thing inside of Cody. A darkness the other brothers didn't have or didn't lean into the way Dev and Cody did, or had. That darker side had almost gotten Dev killed years ago—and Cody had vowed to hone it into a different kind of weapon.

It was a little harder these days now that he was back at the ranch after his last mission with the North Star group. Too many truths about his involvement in the secretive operation had been revealed.

He missed North Star and his confidential work there. It had become vital to the man he'd built himself into. But he'd also been very aware his time with North Star was temporary, just as everyone else's was. It was what made the group effective in taking down large, dangerous organizations.

Like his father's.

The Sons of the Badlands hadn't exactly disbanded last month when their leader had been arrested and their second-in-command had been killed. But they were weaker.

Cody had to let other people dismantle the remaining membership. While he sat on the sidelines herding cattle with his brother.

It just about ate him alive.

He glanced over at Dev, who was rubbing down his horse after an afternoon in the saddle moving the cattle to their new pasture, his two ranch dogs at his feet. Dev kept his expression carefully blank, but even if Cody hadn't been around much the past few years he knew that meant Dev was in some serious pain.

"So, he's really going to stay there?" Dev asked.

Cody didn't ask for clarification. As weeks passed, they all waited for word that Ace would somehow wiggle out of a trial or sentencing. But he was in jail at least.

"For now."

Dev made a considering snort. The dogs sniffed the air, cocked their heads, then both got onto their feet and loped out of the barn. Cody figured Grandma had put some scraps in their bowls.

Dev squinted toward the horizon. Three figures on horseback were coming closer. Duke Knight and his two daughters. Well, Rachel was his biological daughter, Sarah was one of his fosters. The only one he and his wife had managed to legally adopt before Eva Knight had died.

Sometimes Cody thought losing Mrs. Knight had been the beginning of all their problems—even though the real start was the moment they'd been born to Ace Wyatt, head of the Sons of the Badlands.

Thanks to Jamison, Cody had had a pretty normal childhood, getting out of the gang just shy of his seventh birthday. He'd also had his brothers. The Knights had been the kind of ranching neighbors that were more like family. All their daughters—fosters or biological—had been the Wyatt brothers' playmates.

Sometimes more. As had been the case with Liza and Jamison, before Liza had run back to the Sons.

Then later, Cody and Nina.

Cody didn't think about Nina much anymore. He'd erased her from his mind. Or had, until he had to come home.

She seemed to exist like a ghost here at the ranch. All the what-ifs. All the whys.

But it didn't matter. She'd left him. Disappeared and begged him not to follow.

So he hadn't.

"Guess they're coming over for dinner," Cody forced himself to say. It wasn't easy to sit in Grandma's kitchen with Duke Knight, who still blamed him for Nina's disappearing act.

But they pretended it didn't matter, because otherwise Grandma would whack them both with her biggest wooden spoon.

"Not normal," Dev replied.

Which was when Grandma appeared in the barn. But she wasn't dressed to work, and she looked pale.

"Come inside, Cody."

He shared a look with Dev, who shrugged. Grandma seemed grave, which wasn't like her. She usually gave orders with an ornery glint in her eye. This was muted.

Cody had learned a long time ago not to react to most situations. He'd interned in the CIA, and he'd been trained by the North Star group. Not to mention how much he'd learned from looking up to Jamison, who might have saved Cody from the Sons at seven, but had been stuck there until he himself was eighteen.

Cody couldn't access all that training and habit in the face of his very grave grandmother. He was stiff as something like fear actually made his heart beat too hard in his chest.

Still, Cody followed her toward the house. When he saw the ambulance lights he hurried to it, passing up Grandma's slower gait. A woman was on a stretcher being loaded up into the emergency vehicle.

A woman whose face had him stopping in his tracks.

Grandma caught up to him, sounding a little out of breath.

"Why is Ni—" Before he could say her name, Grandma hit him. Hard.

The EMT closed the doors and Cody stared at his grandmother.

"I'll explain soon enough. She isn't who you need to see right this moment," she said, somehow graver than she'd been. Cody might not understand what was going on, but he understood what his grandmother wasn't saying.

That was Nina, and she was in danger. The less talk right now, the better to assess the danger.

"I've already called Gage," Grandma said. "He'll take care of everything at the hospital, but she was hurt too badly for me to patch up. She needed a hospital."

Cody stood, frozen in the spot even as the ambulance began to pull away. Maybe his eyes were playing tricks on him. Maybe that wasn't Nina. Maybe…

"Follow me."

Grandma strode into the house and Cody didn't know what else to do but follow. The sight of Nina, pale and bloody, made it feel as though his brain had short-circuited. Nothing made sense, and all he could do was follow his grandmother into the house.

Through the kitchen, up the stairs, then to the room Liza and her half sister, Gigi, stayed in when they came to visit.

Liza and Gigi weren't there. They'd moved into a house in Bonesteel with Jamison, but another little girl was. She was huddled in the corner, clutching a doll. A doll that had blood on it. Just like her clothes.

"She's unhurt," Grandma said, just standing in the doorway with him.

"Who is she?" he asked, though something felt all wrong. Something clawed at him, dark and painful.

"Nina knocked on my door. She'd been hurt—there was so much blood I called 911 right away. I tried to help her, but she'd been shot in the stomach. I couldn't fix that. Not the way she was bleeding."

"Who is this, Grandma?" Cody reiterated, though the idea of Nina being shot in the stomach… What on earth had she gotten herself into?

"Nina said I needed to hide her," Grandma said, nodding to the girl. "No matter what, I needed to hide her. She just kept begging me not to let anyone know she was alive."

"I don't understand."

"I think you do, Cody. The last thing Nina told me before she passed out was that the child's name is Brianna. And that *you* had to protect her."

The little girl looked up at him with scared eyes and a bloodstained face. She looked vaguely familiar, but Cody couldn't place her. Not with the way his heart thundered in his ears and his body felt like lead.

"She won't let me touch her," Grandma said sadly.

"What makes you think she'll let me?" Cody managed to croak. Even knowing what his grandmother would say, sensing what all this meant, he couldn't get his brain to jump into gear. Couldn't seem to add up all the facts laid before him.

Grandma shook her head. "You're her father, Cody. I'm about sure."

NINA OAKS STRUGGLED to swim out of the black. There was beeping, and her baby was not here with her.

Brianna. Brianna.

Take care of her. He has to protect her.

When she opened her eyes, there were familiar ones staring back at her.

But not the ones she'd expected to see. Or maybe *hoped* to. Maybe someday she'd learn how not to hope, but she was beginning to doubt it.

She remembered, suddenly, everything. The break-in. The masked man. Hiding Brianna.

The masked man had shot her, but then she'd managed…

She closed her eyes against the memory. She'd been shot. She was in a hospital. And Brianna…

"Gage," she croaked. She supposed any Wyatt brother would do, even if it wasn't the one she really needed to talk to. They knew her. They'd protect her. They were her only hope.

"Hello, Mal."

She scrunched her face up against the pain, and the wave of confusion. "That's not my name. Gage, you know who—"

He placed his hand very gently on her arm that had an IV hooked up to it. "I know your name is Malory Jones," he said, his gaze on her, his words rote and devoid of emotion. "I found you on the side of the road. We're going to get you patched up. Don't you worry."

That wasn't what happened, but even in her foggy brain she knew better than to argue with him. He looked bigger than she remembered, but she supposed it was just the uniform. She was used to seeing him at Grandma Pauline's. Not in tiny hospital rooms.

Malory Jones.

He knew who she was. She had to believe Gage knew who she was. It hadn't been that long. Only about seven years. She hadn't changed. Not really. Not to look at anyway.

"I don't remember…" She had to remember things. Get everything sorted in her head so she could make a plan. So she could…

Brianna. He has to keep her safe.

"That's all right. It'll be clearer when you're not getting pumped full of drugs. Right now you just keep quiet and focus on healing. Quiet is the best thing, *Mal.*"

He was keeping her identity a secret. She couldn't quite remember things. "Gage, I need to know..." Even with what she couldn't remember, she knew she couldn't utter Brianna's name. She had to keep her daughter's existence a secret.

But she desperately had to know Brianna was all right. Nina remembered being shot. She dimly remembered grabbing a jagged piece of the lamp that had been broken and using all her strength to lodge it in her attacker's neck.

She remembered the blood, and his screams, and she remembered crawling to Brianna's bed and getting her daughter out of the house before anyone else could come after them.

Then she'd had to burn it down, to keep Brianna's existence a secret. Burning it all away to cinders was the only way to escape the Sons' detection.

"Gage... Gage... Please." She felt a tear trickle down her cheek. She didn't remember past the fire. She didn't remember where Brianna was.

Gage crouched down so he was eye level with her as she lay in the hospital bed. "Listen. Everyone's fine and safe now. We'll get you patched up." He reached out and brushed the tear away. "Everyone is fine. *Everyone*. Okay?"

He meant Brianna. He had to mean her. She nodded. She tried to breathe and believe. She would do anything for her baby. Suffer anything. Nina had to believe she'd gotten Brianna to safety.

To the Wyatts.

Cody. She was almost certain she hadn't seen Cody.

And almost certain she wouldn't be able to avoid that eventuality. Or what it meant.

He wouldn't understand. She wanted him to be able to, but he wouldn't. He was too good and brave and sure. He'd believe he would have been able to stop everything and that she should have come to him.

Nina didn't believe that, even now. Even coming to him and his family and tasking them with keeping her daughter safe.

Cody would be dead if not for her. Brianna would be dead if Nina hadn't done what she'd done.

Cody would never forgive her, and she would never be able to believe it could have been different.

The door opened and both her and Gage looked over to the man who stepped into the room.

Furious energy pumped off him. Tall and rangy and ready to attack. She should have been afraid.

But she'd seen all of that in him all those years ago—loved his dark side and being the one to lighten it.

There'd be no soothing anymore.

"I need to talk to her," Cody ground out as Gage slowly got to his feet.

Gage moved in front of Cody, trying to block his route to her bed. "Not here," Gage said, putting a hand on Cody's chest. "Not now."

Cody's hazel eyes blazed with furious, righteous anger. She would have expected nothing less.

Still, she closed her eyes and let the encroaching black win rather than face it. And him.

Chapter Two

Grandma had told him not to come, but after hours of getting nowhere with the little girl, Cody hadn't been able to stop himself. There had to be an explanation. It had to…

It couldn't be true.

But Nina had looked at him when he'd walked into her hospital room, pain in her expression. And something that wasn't apology but was close enough it was hard to deny Grandma's interpretation of the situation.

The little girl who wouldn't let anyone wash the blood off her was his.

His.

And Nina had kept her from him. For seven years.

Gage nudged him out of the room and Cody let himself be led because she'd closed her eyes anyway. Not in a pretend kind of way. In an unconscious kind of way.

"Go home, Cody. I'll take care of things here."

Cody wanted to laugh. Take care of things. What was there to take care of? What did any of this *mean*?

"The more you stay, the more you give away. Which

means the more danger she is in," Gage said in a fierce whisper. "I know you don't want that."

"I don't know what I want."

"As soon as she's able to be moved, she will be. Just leave. We have to be careful right now."

"Why are we acting like—"

"What exactly do you think a woman—your ex-girlfriend—showing up at the ranch with a bullet hole in her body means, Cody?"

"He's in jail," Cody returned in the same guttural whisper his brother was speaking in. "And we're in a hospital so I don't—"

"He's in jail. They *all* aren't. Someone put a bullet in her. Someone who's likely still looking for her. Whatever secrets—"

"Yeah, she's got some secrets all right."

"Look. I only know what Grandma told me. I can't imagine… I'm not saying you don't have a right to be angry. I'm not saying you shouldn't want answers. I'm saying this isn't just delicate, it's dangerous." Gage put his hand on Cody's shoulder, as if he could steady him through this. "Not just for you. For all of us."

"What would you have me do?" Cody ground out.

"Go home. Watch over everything there. I'll handle this, and when she can be moved, we'll figure it all out."

Cody hated that answer. He wanted to argue with Gage. He wanted to install himself in Nina's hospital room and demand all the answers he needed.

But Gage was right. Cody couldn't find a way to outreason everything Gage had said.

"Go home, Cody."

Cody turned and did just that. It didn't seem to matter—all the rage and fury inside of him had frozen at the sight of Nina pale in that hospital bed looking at him like he was her absolute worst nightmare.

And her total salvation.

He drove back to the ranch in that frozen state. The name Brianna kept circling around his head, but he couldn't seem to put together a discernible thought.

When he walked back into the ranch kitchen, Grandma was at the sink, washing dishes.

"You should be in bed," Cody said, noting that it was nearly midnight. Hours upon hours of…

"She keeps hiding under the bed any time the door opens or closes," Grandma said on a sigh, ignoring his admonition. "I called all the girls—out of desperation." She turned off the water and proceeded to dry her hands on a kitchen towel. "She hides. She's good at hiding, but all the girls are up there now doing what they can."

The girls. Duke Knight's army of daughters. Up there with—

With…

"Cody. Whatever this is. Whatever has happened. You need to put it away. Your feelings don't matter until that little girl is safe."

"That little girl…" Cody closed his eyes. He couldn't believe she was his. Couldn't believe Nina would hurt him that way. She'd broken up with him all those years ago, but he hadn't been surprised by that. Nina had always been sweet, good. He was not that. No good for her—Duke Knight had always been sure to tell them both.

He'd been at his CIA internship and she'd left him a message that it was over. It had hurt. It had been out of the blue, but in the end, it had only seemed right.

So, no, losing Nina hadn't been any big surprise. But this?

This was bigger than anything. Than everything.

A daughter. His.

Couldn't be true.

"Go up there. Talk to her. See if you can figure out what's going on without scaring her."

Cody could have argued. He almost wanted to. But they needed to know what was going on, and Brianna seemed to be the best option.

"Be quiet though," Grandma ordered. "Gigi is asleep in my room."

Cody nodded and headed upstairs. When he reached Liza and Gigi's usual room, all the lights were blazing. Every Knight girl past and present was assembled in the room, Brianna in the center.

The blood was gone. Her hair was damp so they must have given her a bath. She was wearing some too-big clothes, but she looked... Tired, but also calm.

"You got her to take a bath."

All heads turned to him, even Brianna's. Her eyes were blue, like her mother's. But instead of Nina's light blond hair, her flyaway strands were a dark brown. Like his.

She didn't look like either of them fully and yet somehow he knew...

"Once we all showed up, she decided to give it a go," Liza offered, a small, sad smile on her face.

"Because they're the princesses," Brianna said. "I knew I was safe with the princesses, and they said Mommy will be okay."

Cody gave Sarah a questioning look, but she didn't say anything while Rachel held the girl in her lap and Liza braided her hair.

"The princesses?" Cody questioned, still standing in the doorway to the room.

"Mommy used to tell me about the princesses. Princess Rachel can't see very well," she said, reaching up to the scar across Rachel's eye that had been put there by a cougar when Rachel had been little. Brianna touched the lighter skin and the darker skin gently, reverently before turning to the other women around her.

"Princess Sarah doesn't want to be a princess. She wants to be a knight. She's a warrior." Brianna smiled at Sarah, who wasn't dressed so much as a warrior or a knight as she was a rancher, but it didn't seem to make much difference to the six-year-old.

"Princess Cecilia always wanted a badge." Brianna pointed to Cecilia's tribal police badge, since Cecilia was still in uniform. She must have come straight from her shift at the reservation.

"Princess Felicity protects the animals and the forests." Felicity didn't have her park ranger uniform on, but she had clearly had some kind of conversation about it with Brianna.

"What about Liza?" Cody heard himself ask, feeling unbalanced and yet firmly rooted to the spot. To her blue eyes.

"She's not a princess." Brianna smiled big and wide. "She's the queen who keeps everyone safe, even when she was far away."

Liza finished the braid as she gave Cody a heart-breaking look filled with tears that didn't fall.

"And who am I?" Cody asked, his voice cracking somewhere in the middle of that question, though he barely even noticed it. He felt fuzzy and distant.

Brianna cocked her head and studied him. "You're my daddy. But you don't know I'm your daughter, because the bad men made us run away. Even brave knights need help sometimes."

"What bad men?"

Brianna kept her gaze on his, but there was no more smiling. "All of them."

"I NEED YOU to get me out of here."

Gage, who had barely left her hospital room as far as Nina knew these past few days, gave her a doleful look.

Nina sat up in the bed, ignoring the pain in her body. "I'm okay. I know I'm not good but I'm good enough to get out. I have to. I *have* to."

"You were shot in the stomach."

"And they've stitched me up. Gage. I can't just lie here much longer. I need…" She didn't want to say it. They avoided the topic of Brianna. Nina knew her daughter was safe with the Wyatts, but that was all she knew. That was *all* she knew.

For seven years—since she'd found out she was

pregnant—she had existed solely to take care of Brianna. To keep her safe and healthy and completely off the Sons' radar.

I need Brianna.

Brianna needs me.

Even though she knew her strong, amazing girl was being taken care of by Grandma Pauline and the Wyatt brothers. Probably Duke and the girls too.

Her heart ached—there was something painful about Brianna meeting them all without Nina there to be with her.

Still, Brianna knew about them. About Nina's foster parents who'd given her a real home. Love and safety and three square meals. School and chores and a real life. Brianna knew about Nina's sisters—sort of.

Nina had always made it sound like a fairy tale so if Brianna ever talked about them to strangers, people would think they were fictional. But Nina had given her daughter stories of the people who'd given Nina the kind of life she'd never even dreamed of when she'd been growing up poor and hungry in her biological parents' drug-infested trailer.

Her sisters, the princesses. And the brave Wyatt brothers, knights in shining armor.

"I need to get out," she repeated to Gage.

"I'll see what I can do, but I need you to know everything is fine."

She wanted to tell him it wasn't, but he couldn't understand. He wasn't a parent. He didn't know what it was like to…

She remembered more and more every day. Killing

the man who'd shot her. Driving as far as she could with a towel wrapped around her bleeding midsection. Then walking when she'd been afraid she'd crash the car. Brianna in her arms, trudging toward the one place she knew she could find help.

She didn't remember Grandma Pauline or the ambulance ride and wondered if she ever would.

It didn't matter.

She'd gotten her baby to safety, and Gage seemed to understand how important it was for no one to know Brianna was alive. For no one to know who Nina really was.

The longer she stayed, the easier it would be for someone to figure it out. Surely the people who'd tried to kill her knew she was hurt, and if they were who she thought they were…

They'd start looking into the Wyatts. Probably already had.

"We're not safe. The longer it goes on. I have to get—"

Gage gave her a sharp look. "We've got it covered. Trust me."

"Please." She knew crying wouldn't sway him one way or another. Not because he was cruel or unaffected by tears, but because—unless things had changed in the past seven years—the Wyatt brothers were actually quite uncomfortable with a woman's tears, something they couldn't fix or control.

But Gage took the seat next to her bed and leaned forward. "Do you think I don't understand? That I don't know exactly what they're capable of? I may not know why they decided to target you after so long, but I know what all of this is. Everyone is being kept as safe as possible."

She wished she could explain to him it wasn't a lack of trust or belief. It was just she *needed* to see her daughter. She needed to hold Brianna and tell her things would be all right. She needed the time she hadn't had after she'd been shot to explain to Brianna that everything was going to be okay.

But Nina didn't have the words and when the door opened she could only sag in her bed as one of the nurses peeked her head in. "Mrs. Jones? Your husband and daughter are here."

Nina sat back up, wincing at the pain in her side. "My…"

Cody stepped inside. He had a hat pulled low and was different than he'd been the other day, but she could hardly notice it because he was carrying a little girl with red hair.

"Do you need another dose of pain—"

"No," Nina snapped, because it was taking everything in her power to keep from sobbing and jumping from the bed. Even with a wig and ill-fitting clothes, she knew that bundle. "I'm all right."

The nurse nodded and stepped back out. Before Nina could say anything, before she could hold her arms out for Brianna to come to her, Cody shook his head sharply. He nodded to Gage. "Watch the door."

Gage was clearly not in on this, or in approval. He stood slowly. "Cody?"

"I've got it covered. Watch the door."

Gage scowled at his brother's order, but something

passed between them and he eventually nodded and stepped outside.

Cody didn't say anything. He began to prowl the room, inspecting things, putting little devices on the walls, all while carrying Brianna. Who didn't say a word. Who held on to Cody like he'd always been her very-present father.

But the whole time, Brianna's eyes stayed on Nina. So she smiled. Big and wide with so much pride and love for her girl.

Nina watched as Cody kept moving around. "What are you—"

He held his finger to his lips and kept doing things she couldn't see or understand. Once he was satisfied with *whatever*, he crossed to the bed and sat Brianna down on the side of it.

Nina grabbed Brianna so fiercely the wig tumbled off, but it didn't matter. Brianna wrapped her arms around Nina's neck, and no matter that Nina's whole body hurt, she didn't adjust Brianna's grip.

"Oh, my baby. Baby girl." She couldn't say all the things she wanted to say. Apologies. Questions. Too many sobs clogged her throat. She couldn't let those out, so she just held on.

"Are you going to die?" Brianna whispered. "Daddy said no, but I want you to tell me."

Daddy. Twin feelings paralyzed Nina. A joyous relief that finally Brianna knew her father. A cold fear that… That they'd always be in danger from here on out.

Too late now.

Nina tugged Brianna's arms off her neck so she could look in her child's familiar blue eyes. "I am not going to die. The doctors fixed me up. I have to heal, but I'm not going to die." *Not here. Not now.* She looked up at Cody. "*Daddy* is right about that."

Chapter Three

It was hard enough to handle how easily Brianna had started calling him Daddy. She had no qualms, no questions. Because Nina had told Brianna about him, and so Brianna recognized him as the man from her mother's stories. She trusted her mother's stories.

Cody hadn't been told anything. Somehow he already loved that little girl after a few short days, but that didn't make it easy or simple to wrap his head around the facts.

It was just the way it was. What was he going to do? Tell a six-year-old to not call him that? She called him Daddy and he answered and his own feelings on the matter would be dealt with internally and in his own time.

But Nina looking at him while she called Cody Brianna's daddy broke something inside of him. He didn't know what, or how to fix it. He could only stare at her and wonder… How…

How?

He'd wanted to come alone, but Brianna needed some reassurances. While the "princesses," as she called the Knight girls, had opened her up some, enough to let them all take care of her—anxiety crept in with every passing hour she didn't see Nina.

So he'd brought her. Now he didn't know what to do. Not a sensation he was used to.

But he'd searched for listening devices, installed a few frequency busters in case someone was trying to listen in. No one could hear them in this room while they discussed this, so discuss it they would.

Before he could figure out what question to ask first, Nina pinned him with a desperate look.

"Cody, you have to get me out of here. It's too dangerous. They're looking for me."

"Who's looking for you?" he asked, trying to access his old self. The self that had investigated mysteries and ordered missions. An old self that didn't get emotionally involved in cases even when they involved his father or the Sons.

"Who do you think?" Nina replied, still holding on to Brianna with a death grip.

"Why would the Sons be after you after so long?"

"Cody…" Her eyebrows drew together, as if he was the one missing information. "They've always been after me."

"What does that mean?"

She let out a shaky breath. "I…" She glanced nervously at Brianna. "Back then…"

"We can talk about it later." As much because he didn't want Brianna overhearing things that would hurt her or scare her as the fact he didn't want…

He didn't want to have to go back over that breakup

seven years ago and see all the signs he must have missed. All the things he'd ignored because he'd been hurt. Because it was becoming increasingly clear to him that the breakup seven years ago hadn't been as *inevitable* as he'd assumed.

"You need to get me out," Nina said in a fierce whisper. "You need to."

"Ace is in jail."

Again confusion took over her features. "How can that… How can that be? It was one of his men who shot me."

"You're sure?"

"Yes." When he kept his gaze steady on her she wilted a little. "No. I mean, I didn't see him. He was dressed…" Again she looked at Brianna, clearly not wanting to get too far into it. "Who else, Cody? Who else?"

"I don't know what you've been doing these past few years."

The hurt that chased over her face was too hard to watch, so he turned his attention to Brianna. "We need to go."

"I don't want to."

"I know, but your mom needs to sleep to get better."

"I'll sleep with her."

Cody had to scrub his hands over his face. What had Nina gotten him into? Them all into?

Was it Nina, or was it you?

"Grandma Pauline was going to make a cake," Cody managed to say, though he had to admit he didn't sound very excited about it.

Nina rolled her eyes at him, but when she turned her attention to Brianna, she smiled big and bright. "Go on. I'm going to get better as soon as possible." Nina picked up the wig she'd knocked off Brianna's head. "And you get to play dress up and eat cake," Nina said, fixing the wig back on.

"The princesses gave me new toys."

"The..." Nina smiled, though it was sad around the edges. "And they'll protect you." Nina looked up at Cody, something indescribable in her expression. "And so will all those brave knights."

"You need a knight," Brianna said, her forehead pleated with worry.

"I have one," Nina replied easily, still smiling. Cody wondered if Brianna saw through it as easily as he did. "The man who was in here when you got here? That's your daddy's big brother. He's been keeping me safe, and he's going to keep doing that. Okay?"

"Why aren't *you* keeping Mommy safe?" Brianna asked, frowning at Cody.

Cody found himself speechless, which wasn't something he'd ever had a problem with until the past few days. But his daughter looking at him with such accusation when he hadn't even fully come to grips with the fact he *had* a daughter.

"Your daddy's job is to keep *you* safe," Nina said. She looked up at him, imploring and desperate. "And to get me out of here as soon as he can."

Cody didn't appreciate being put on the spot like that, but he was beginning to—somewhat against his will—come to her way of thinking. If it was the Sons who'd hurt her, for whatever reason, it wouldn't take much longer for them to come sniffing around the Wyatts, and it would eventually lead them to this hospital.

"We'll do our best. All us knights." Cody forced himself to smile and hold out his arms for Brianna. She gave Nina a kiss on the cheek and one last squeeze, then reluctantly went to him.

"Can't I walk?" she whined.

"We're trying to keep your age a secret, remember?" Brianna sighed. "I'm tired of secrets," she mumbled.

Cody didn't say anything, but he met Nina's gaze. Regret. Fear. Sadness. Hurt.

It all echoed inside of him. So he turned away. "We'll do our best," he muttered, opening the door. As he stepped out, he pulled his hat back low and looked at Gage, who was standing there guarding the door, thank God.

"What do you know?" Cody asked Gage on a whisper.

"She's been living in Dyner," Gage said, keeping his voice low and their heads bent together.

Dyner was a small town at the edge of Valiant County. She'd been that close. *That* close. Granted, Cody had been living in Wyoming so it wasn't as if they would have run into each other, but…

"She killed a man—the man who shot her. He was a member of the Sons. It's not going to take long for one of the nurses to put it together when Tucker comes to investigate."

"He can't—"

"Why do you think he hasn't yet? But this is his job,

Cody. He's the detective. He can only bend so many rules without losing his badge."

Rules. It was why Cody hadn't been able to follow his brothers' footsteps. He'd wanted to be a cop too, except for the rules. They too often didn't help people who needed to be helped.

Cody looked down at Brianna in his arms. She had her head leaned against his shoulder. She wasn't crying, but she looked like she might start at any moment. "We have to get her out."

Gage pulled a face, but he didn't argue. "Got any bright ideas?"

"Not yet, but we act now. One way or another."

NINA HAD BEEN brought up by the Knights to believe in right and wrong. Good people followed the rules and the world would reward them if they did.

She didn't believe that anymore. Seven years of keeping her daughter's identity a secret, of moving and hiding and living in fear would shatter anyone's fairy-tale views.

Sneaking out of the hospital was wrong, and it felt wrong, but she knew she had to do it. Gage had created a slight diversion, and Cody had taken out her IV and done something to the equipment so it wouldn't alert the nurses she'd removed the ports.

Then Cody had left with Brianna, leaving Nina to find a way to sneak out as soon as Gage gave her the go-ahead signal.

The Wyatt boys had made it easy, and she'd walked

right out of the small local hospital as if she was actually supposed to.

When she saw Cody standing next to a truck, his hat pulled low, pretending to puff on a cigarette, her heart beat hard against her ribs reminding her she was alive.

No matter the aches, the pains, the fear that she actually wouldn't survive all this, she was alive. She had to keep living and trying for Brianna, no matter what hurt—body or heart.

He opened the passenger side door for her, dropping the unlit cigarette and crushing it with his boot. She slid inside and smiled back at Brianna in the back. Somehow they'd found a booster seat for her.

"How…"

Cody slid into the driver's side seat. "It's Gigi's. Uh, Gigi is Liza's little sister. She's only four, so we had to adjust it for Brianna, but it worked for today."

"Liza. I haven't seen her…" It had only been Nina's second year with the Knights when Liza had come to live with them. Liza had been sixteen, and the Knight girls had all been significantly younger. There'd been a big uproar because she and the oldest Wyatt boy had finally gotten out of the Sons.

Nina remembered that summer. Remembered how scared she'd been that if the Knights added another girl, they might send her back.

Nina had been the last foster, and the other girls had been together for years before the Knights had asked her to come home with them. But Nina had been afraid. Afraid to get too close. To settle in.

Then Liza had come and made Nina even more

afraid. But instead of sending Nina back, or having less room, something about Liza had made them a family. A real family.

Then Liza had disappeared three years later. Back to the Sons everyone said. But Nina had known she'd only gone back to save her sister Marci. No matter what the Wyatt brothers had thought.

"Liza's back then."

"More or less. She lives in Bonesteel with her little sister and Jamison."

"Jamison. But…" Jamison had been the most devastated by Liza's disappearance. And the most angry. Granted that was all fifteen years ago.

Cody shrugged. "Got back together last month when she left the Sons."

The words *got back together* hung between them, heavy and uncomfortable as Cody pulled out of the hospital parking lot.

"Gage will stay back for a few hours," Cody said, his voice cool and devoid of emotion. "Then he'll make an excuse that he got a call, but not to bother you. It should buy us some hours."

"But they know Gage. They know you."

"If it's the Sons, they know us anyway. If it's not? That'll take longer."

"It's the Sons," Nina said flatly.

He shifted a glance in the rearview mirror, so Nina did the same. Brianna was fast asleep.

"She hasn't done much of that," Cody said. "She wouldn't do anything until the girls—the *princesses*—all got there. They gave her a bath and she ate a bit.

She's very talkative and seems…okay, but she's not sleeping or eating enough. She's been too worried."

Nina nodded, her stomach tying in knots. "We can't stay at the ranch."

"You can. You will."

"Cody—"

"You came to us for a reason, Nina. I assume in part because it's my fault if the Sons are trying to hurt you. But also because you knew we could keep you both safe. You're going to have to trust me to make those decisions. And my decision is you're at the ranch for the time being."

"You still think you're invincible," she said, before she could think better of it and temper the bitterness out of her tone.

He gave her an enigmatic look before turning his attention back to the road. "No one's invincible. But some people will do whatever it takes to make things right. *Whatever* it takes."

Chapter Four

Nina had kept it together. For Brianna's sake. For her own. Because letting her guard down with Cody would surely mean all kinds of trouble.

But when Cody pulled up to Grandma Pauline's ranch, and Duke Knight stood there waiting, she absolutely lost it.

He'd been her one true father figure, and she didn't realize until this moment how desperately she'd missed having someone to lean on. Someone who loved her, no matter what. A strong, sure presence. Always.

Brianna was still asleep so Nina let herself cry as she got out of the car and practically ran for him. He met her halfway, enveloping her in a tight hug. It didn't matter that her stomach hurt. He still smelled like horses and leather and home.

When he pulled her back, his dark eyes were full of tears. "You're lucky you're still healing, girlie, because I have a heap of lectures waiting for you."

His voice had gone raspier, and there was more gray at his temples than there had been. He was the absolute best man she knew. From taking her in when she'd been a shy little mess, to keeping all his daughters—biological and foster—strong and whole through Liza running away, and then his beloved wife dying shortly after.

Breaking up with Cody had been hard, but leaving her family had been a sacrifice she probably wouldn't have been able to bear... If she hadn't found out she was pregnant. It had made the ache for home greater, but it had made the stakes so much higher.

"Took three of us just to keep him from charging off to the hospital."

Nina inhaled and turned to find Dev. She let out a breath. Seven years had changed him. Not for the better. He was skinnier, edgier. She'd watched him slowly climb out of the near-death experience he'd suffered ten years ago, but it had left a forever mark that only seemed to deepen with time.

"Hi, Dev."

"Let's get inside," Cody said. "We can't be too careful."

Nina managed to look at him. Brianna was curled up against him. He made carrying her look easy when she was having a harder and harder time hefting Brianna's ever-growing frame.

Nina doubted inside was any safer than outside. If the Sons had finally come after her, it was because of her connection to the Wyatts. Grandma Pauline's ranch would be the first place they looked.

She let Cody usher her inside as Brianna yawned and woke up. With time to think more than panic, Nina could see that her coloring had been off, but the nap in the car had helped some.

"Come here, baby." Nina held out her arms.

Cody shook his head. "You're not supposed to be carrying anything."

She opened her mouth to argue, but there were too many men in the kitchen looking at her like she'd break.

Grandma Pauline bustled into the kitchen. "Now, you'll sit and you'll eat," she said by way of greeting, already making a beeline for the stove. Though she patted Nina's shoulder as she passed—which was often as close to a hug as Grandma Pauline ever got.

Slowly, Nina lowered herself into a chair at the kitchen table. She placed her palms on the scarred wood. Grandma Pauline's table had been a second home, which had been a miracle for a girl who'd been born into such a terrible one. To be brought to a place surrounded by so many people who cared. So many places to go when she was afraid or upset or lonely.

To have to leave it, all because she'd fallen in love. Even after seven years of living on the run, she couldn't find a way to make herself believe it had been a mistake. That she'd fallen in love with the wrong person. Cody had understood her better than anyone back then. And he'd given her Brianna.

The child he was setting down on the ground, as if he'd been born to be a father to her wonderful girl.

Brianna crossed the floor and seated herself on Nina's lap. Nina held her close and tight and tried to breathe through all the horrible and wonderful things pressing against her chest.

"Have you met Duke?" Nina asked Brianna through a tight throat, turning Brianna to face where Duke took a seat next to her.

Duke nodded slowly and Brianna bounced in Nina's lap, causing Nina to wince in pain.

"Grandpa Duke already gave me a present," Brianna said happily through bites of a cookie Grandma Pauline had sneaked her somehow.

"Grandpa," Nina echoed, touched beyond measure. Duke was her daughter's grandfather. It opened up a yawning, painful regret she knew would eat her alive if she'd let it.

It *hurt* that she'd lost her family seven years ago, but she had to remember why she'd done it. To save Cody. To save Brianna. She couldn't focus on the regret. She had to focus on the present.

Getting out of the hospital had been a start, but if the Sons suddenly wanted her dead—whether because they'd finally tracked her down or for some other reason—they wouldn't stop. Even if Ace was in jail, which she didn't quite believe.

The only way they'd stop now that they'd shot her was if they thought she'd died in that fire.

All things Nina didn't want to discuss in front of Brianna, no matter how much Brianna had gleaned from living her entire life knowing bad men were after them.

At the sound of little feet, Nina turned to the entryway of the kitchen that led out into the living room. A little girl scurried in, grinning broadly at everyone.

Behind her at a slower pace, a tall brunette appeared.

"Oh my God," Nina breathed. Cody had mentioned Liza, but Nina didn't know how to handle these onslaughts of memory and reality.

Brianna slid off Nina's lap and ran over to the little girl standing next to Liza. The two girls hugged like they were the best of friends and Nina could only stare at Liza. They'd been sisters for such a short time, but she supposed time didn't matter when you'd grown up with so few people in your life who'd loved you or cared about your well-being. The ones who did, no matter for how long, mattered.

Nina slowly got to her feet, in part because this all felt so surreal and in part because her side hurt.

"You've looked better, kid," Liza said, her voice scratchy at best.

Much like with Duke outside, Nina didn't try to hold herself back. She moved forward and grabbed onto Liza, squeezing as tight as possible. She let it all go. Let herself remember what it was like to have a family, to depend on someone else.

Liza's arms were gentle, likely she was being careful because of Nina's injuries. Liza was older, and she'd always seemed to know everything. Looking back, Nina knew it wasn't true, but she wanted to believe in Liza's all-knowing powers for a while.

Liza cleared her throat and pulled away. "I'll watch the girls. You all have your war council. Then we can catch up."

Nina looked back at the table where Duke, Dev,

Cody and Grandma Pauline were now seated, looking very much like just that—a *war* council. She let out a shaky breath.

For seven years she'd run. She knew that coming home to the Wyatts would mean only one thing.

Now it was time to fight.

CODY HAD NOW watched Nina fall apart while facing two people from her past.

She hadn't fallen apart when she'd seen him in that hospital room—him, the person she'd kept their daughter a secret from for so long.

It burned. Brianna being kept from him for so long was the kind of betrayal a person didn't just *set aside*.

Unless said daughter was in mortal danger, he supposed.

So, no. Betrayal couldn't be focused on right now. Survival came first—it always did. He might have been saved from the Sons at the age of six, but he'd always known the cost and importance of survival.

Nina returned to her seat at the table, wincing as she sat. Whether out of pain or the fact everyone's attention was on her as Liza led the girls out of the kitchen with the promise of a tea party.

Nina inhaled and let the breath out slowly. He knew he should speak first. Lay out what they knew, but all he could seem to do was stare at her. She looked exactly the same. Same freckles, same dark blue eyes. Her hair was a little longer than it had been back then, but other than that, nothing about her had changed.

Except the woman he'd known, would never have kept his own child from him.

Unless she'd finally understood what it meant to be a Wyatt, and that she never wanted that mark on her child.

He had to get his head on straight. Daughter or not, Nina back here or not, there were lives at stake and he'd dedicated his life to saving lives from the Sons. No matter how he felt about said lives.

"We can't stay here," Nina finally said, her expression pained. "They'll already be looking for me here. Gage was in my hospital room. They're not going to view that as coincidence."

Cody looked down at his hands, clenched into fists. Carefully, mindfully, he unclenched his fingers and placed his palm against the scarred wood. "True," he replied evenly. "But they'd have to track you to that hospital. I'm not convinced they did."

"Fine. But they'll check here. You know they will."

He had no doubt, but he had protections for that. Protections he'd made before he'd known Nina had his child.

Your child. Your child.

Daddy.

One by one, he pressed his fingers into the wood, focused on the feel of it. Focused on the smell of Grandma Pauline's chili soup simmering on the stove.

"Why don't you start from the beginning," Duke said gently, and there was a warning in the look he shot Cody.

Cody could look down pure evil, could even hold

his grandmother's censoring gaze most of the time, but he did not know what to do with the *blame* in Duke's dark eyes.

"Which beginning is that?" Nina returned, and her voice was sharp enough he knew without looking her way she was throwing that question at him as a kind of challenge.

"Someone shot you. Start there," Cody replied, facing her with the blankest expression he could muster under the circumstances.

Your daughter. Your daughter.

"I was living in Dyner."

There was a collective noise around the table, almost a sound of pain. Duke and Grandma were horrified she'd been so close. So close and they hadn't known.

"We'd been there about six months," Nina continued. "Brianna needed to start school, and I didn't know where to do it where she'd be safe. Being close seemed the best option. The Sons wouldn't think I'd come back toward home."

It was smart, if a gamble still. But everything about outwitting the Sons was a gamble.

"It had been about two years since I'd had a… run-in, shall we call it. I'd been living in Oklahoma then. Someone broke into my apartment while we were gone. Luckily I…" She trailed off and rubbed her hand against her chest.

Grandma was immediately on her feet, gathering bowls and serving up chili and crackers and glasses of milk. In Grandma's world, the first thing you fixed about a person was the state of their stomach—then they could deal with their emotional affairs.

"The reason I ran in the first place was I knew they could never know Brianna existed. So, I've been very careful. I don't leave evidence of a child around. Brianna learned to put her things in hiding places—not that we ever had many things to begin with. But I just knew... I knew I had to keep her a secret."

Cody wanted to get up out of his seat. He wanted to prowl the kitchen. He wanted to *break* things.

Instead he leaned back casually in his chair. "So what you're telling me is that no one knew Brianna existed—not just me." He shouldn't have said that last part. Not *now*. But...

"Yes, that's what I'm saying," she returned, and her weak attempt at coldness failed miserably. "I hadn't had any run-ins for two years. We were living under a fake name. I worked at a gas station while Brianna was in school. It was a ramshackle little place, family run. They paid me under the table. They were nice. Even let me rent this small house they owned for less than..."

Nina seemed to lose herself in her memories and Cody had to fight against his own impatience.

"I'm sure glad to hear you had some nice people looking after you," Duke said, reaching out and patting Nina's hand. Complete with another glare in Cody's direction.

She smiled. "We've been lucky. Really. Until..." She took a deep breath and looked down at the chili soup Grandma had put in front of her. "Until that night.

Morning I guess, but really early. I heard something—
I thought it was Brianna. She sleepwalks sometimes."

His daughter sleepwalked sometimes. His daughter.
And all she'd had for six years was Nina and danger.

"It wasn't Brianna. It was a man busting in my front
door. He lifted a gun." Nina shuddered. "I did the first
thing I could think of and threw my phone at him.
It must have surprised him enough because the shot
missed me and hit a lamp. It shattered into a million
pieces and I dived to grab a piece of it and hide behind the couch."

Cody did stand then, his chair scraping violently
against the floor. He couldn't...

"Sit down and eat, boy," Grandma ordered sharply.

He only looked at her with one furious sneer. "I
will not. I cannot." He strode for the door. He'd come
back and do his duty, but he needed to pound on *something* first.

"I fought him off, and that's when he shot me. But
I used the shard and jabbed it in his neck. I'm pretty
sure I killed him," Nina said all in a rush, as if hoping to get it all out before he stepped outside. "Then I
grabbed Brianna and set a fire and—"

"You set a *fire*?" Dev asked incredulously.

"I had to hide any sign of Brianna being alive," Nina
replied. "We were careful, but she still existed. If they
came after me, knew it was *me*, and found the rem-
nants of a child... I didn't have time to get her things.
I'd been shot. So, yes, I started a fire."

When Cody turned to look at her, some combina-
tion of shock and horror dulling some of his fury to

just plain confusion, she was looking up at him with what seemed pleading eyes.

But she wasn't begging. She was reciting everything she'd done to keep their daughter alive and unknown to his father's gang.

"Then they still don't know she exists," Dev said.

"I don't think they do. I hope to God they don't." She kept her eyes on Cody the whole time. "Which is why we can't stay here. They will look for me here and they will find her."

Chapter Five

Cody didn't walk out the door as Nina half expected him to. She'd clearly knocked some of the fury out of him by detailing the lengths she'd gone to in keeping Brianna a secret.

But she wasn't so sure this was better. She couldn't work out what stormed in his eyes. It wasn't just anger, and it wasn't just blame. It was oceans of hurt, and Nina didn't know how to fix any of it.

"I need to speak with Nina alone," he finally said, his voice a scrape against the quiet room.

"Hell n—"

Nina reached across to Duke, squeezing his hand. "He's right. We have some things to discuss privately."

"Well, it's not happening now," Duke said, withdrawing his hand and standing. He pointed at Cody, and it was only then Nina realized Duke was holding on to his temper. Barely. "You did this."

Nina tried to protest, but no one was listening to her, least of all Duke and Cody.

"You don't get a second alone with her. You fix my

daughter being in trouble for seven years first. Then you can talk about what *you* need."

"Duke."

He whirled on her, anger and hurt vibrating in his big, tough frame. "Oh no, little girl. I held my tongue back then, but I have learned from my mistakes. One of those was ever letting a Wyatt boy near any of my girls."

"You wait just a second," Grandma Pauline said, getting to her feet.

"I have held my tongue, Pauline, but this is a step too far."

"That girl has been shot—brought her child no one knew about here by the skin of her teeth—and you have no right to stand here and place blame."

"I'll stand here and place blame where it belongs."

Nina seemed to be the only one who noticed Cody slip out the door. Which felt all too much like they were back in high school. Duke had never expressed his displeasure about her dating Cody, but there'd often been fights. Jamison, the oldest Wyatt brother trying to play father to the rest—the rest taking exception—Grandma Pauline wading in and laying down the law.

Cody had never been built for it. He was an introvert, she'd always thought. He had to work his way through his problems on his own. He couldn't shout them out. It just didn't work for him.

She supposed it had been part of the attraction. All she remembered of her parents was dramatic yelling and arguments and blame. A wild, out-of-control abandon to everything.

The Knight house had involved shouting too, though she'd learned to live with it—because the arguments always ended in forgiveness and love. The Wyatt home was always chaos, noise and shouts, but with that same undercurrent of love and caring.

But even when they'd been teenagers Cody had been controlled and separate from that most of the time. She knew he felt deeply, wanted to act, but he contained it all very carefully.

Her heart squeezed as Grandma Pauline and Duke's argument turned into downright hollering. She glanced helplessly at Dev.

Dev nodded to the door, a signal for her to take the escape. He'd stay and clean up the aftermath.

It wasn't the first time Duke and Grandma Pauline had had a heated argument. It wasn't even the most vicious fight she'd watched them have, but it still made Nina's stomach cramp to think it was over her.

She got out of her seat and walked to the door, slipping out of it just as Cody had done. Now they could have their private conversation while the older generation fought over if they should.

Cody was standing over by the barn. He had one booted foot on the lowest rung of one of the pasture fences. He didn't have his hat on, and his dark hair moved with the slight breeze.

Though he didn't move or react to her approach, she knew without a shadow of a doubt he was aware of exactly where she was. She'd seen enough of the "cop" versions of his older brothers to know what that kind of feigned distractedness really meant.

Full and utter attention.

So she decided to speak first even though she didn't know how to broach the subject they really needed to discuss. "I guess we'll always be teenagers to them."

He didn't say anything. If they *were* teenagers, she would have reached out. Brushed her hand down his rigid back. She would have said something soft and sweet to break him out of his solitary brooding.

But they weren't teenagers anymore and she was the cause of his pain. She *knew* she'd never be able to explain it to him in a way he'd accept, but the words bubbled up anyway.

"I didn't have a choice."

He gave her a look so scathing she practically stepped back. She swallowed and recentered. She couldn't make him feel the way she wanted him to. So she'd have to be as honest as she could be and let him figure out how he wanted to feel about it without wishing for a certain reaction.

"I know you'll never believe me. You'll think there was something you could have done to save us, but there wasn't. It was so much better for you not to know—for everyone I love not to know."

"She's my daughter."

"And she knew you. She knew everyone. Kind of."

"But I didn't know her." He turned to her, and everything about him was contained and controlled, except the red-hot fury in his eyes. "I never would have let Ace touch her."

"I couldn't let Ace know she existed, regardless," she responded. She might not have self-righteous rage behind her words, but she had something more important. A desperate love and all-encompassing need to protect her child. *Their* child. "I know that hurts you. I'm sorry it had to, but I absolutely did what had to be done to keep her safe." She could tell him about the threats she'd received, but it wouldn't matter to him right now. She didn't even blame him for that. How could she?

She'd kept Brianna from him for almost seven years, and their daughter was a *joy*.

"She has your cowlick," Nina found herself saying, pointing to the crown of his head. "It's a lot more annoying when you're a girl."

"Do you think this helps?" he demanded, his voice so low and pained it almost sounded like a growl.

She wanted to reach out and touch him and knew she would absolutely in no way, shape, or form be welcome to. "Do you think it hurts?" she asked gently.

He turned away from her. "This *all* hurts."

"I'm sorry. I didn't want to come here."

He whirled on her, that control slipping a small measure. "You think that makes it better? That you didn't *want* our help? That you were shot, and our daughter could have been—"

"She wasn't, was she?" Nina demanded before he could finish all the horrible thoughts she'd entertained herself with in that hospital bed. "Because for seven years my entire being has been about protecting her, including this," she said pointing to her aching stomach. "I took a bullet for that child and I'd take a hell of a lot more."

His eyes flashed with a true violent anger. He lifted his chin and looked at her with a detached disdain that made her shiver. He said nothing.

"You have to understand what this all means. You have to understand that Brianna and I can't stay here."

"For now, it's all you can do." Then he simply walked away, as if that was that.

Nina was left with nothing but an ache so deep that she couldn't even blame it on a gunshot wound.

CODY DIDN'T HAVE a plan yet, but there were some things he had to do. Far away from where anyone could hear him.

He walked into the barn, but then walked right out the other side and kept going. Dev could return any moment to do chores or head out to the pastures. Cody walked toward the far fence that marked off the north side of the property. It was a pretty spring day, but he hardly noticed.

He knew every inch of this land, thought he'd understood every inch of himself. But he felt lost today. In emotion. In fear. He couldn't seem to harness either fully no matter how hard he tried.

You'll think there was something you could have done to save us, but there wasn't.

He would have done anything. Everything. The fact Nina didn't believe that… It shouldn't matter. They'd broken up a long time ago.

But he found himself wondering how much of that had been *her* decision.

He shook that thought away. Clearly she'd found

out she was pregnant and wanted to make sure Ace Wyatt never got near her child. She'd succeeded for six years until somehow, someway, his father had found a way to...

It didn't make sense. Why the Sons would be after her if they didn't know about Brianna? But he had to believe they wouldn't have bothered shooting Nina if they knew Brianna existed.

So what *was* this?

Once he was far enough away from the house and the ranch areas to be sure he wouldn't be overheard, Cody pulled his phone out of his pocket and dialed.

"I'm going to change my number," was the woman's greeting.

"Nothing wrong with checking in."

Shay laughed, and he missed that. Not *her* laugh specifically, but the teamwork that could prompt that reaction out of someone even when nothing was funny. He'd spent the past four years immersed in the world of the North Star group—not the youngest Wyatt brother, not left in the dark.

And for all those years Nina had been running away with *his* daughter.

"Cody, if you check in every five seconds I can't get anything done."

"So, there's been nothing new?"

Shay sighed. "Ace hasn't had any visitors at the jail. No contact as far as we can see, outside of his lawyers. We're watching them too, but so far nothing out of the ordinary. We've been looking into the attack on this Oaks woman, but the fire pretty much took out any evidence."

"No chatter?"

"Nothing. Especially nothing that points to the Sons or Ace."

"It had to be him." Cody *knew* his father was behind this. There were no other options. But without evidence…

"Maybe it was, Cody, but I don't have any evidence. We work with facts. You know that."

"You'll keeping looking?"

There was a pause on the other end, and this was what he was afraid of. Not being part of the group anymore meant he couldn't push for information. North Star might be after taking the Sons down, and they had targeted Cody for a reason—he was a Wyatt.

But that didn't mean they would go after this thread. With Ace in jail, they had bigger leads to follow.

But Cody knew that if someone was after Nina in particular, no matter *who* it was, it linked to him.

"I can keep you up-to-date, Cody, but that's all I can do."

He wanted to press her, but it wouldn't do any good. He understood the North Star group too well. It wasn't personal for them. It couldn't be.

It would just be a hell of a lot easier if he had their help. "Thanks, Shay."

"Stay safe, Cody."

He ended the phone call and blew out a breath. He shared Nina's concerns about them staying here, but until he knew where the threat was coming from—

and with Nina recovering from her injuries—it was safer than running.

Besides, there were *some* protections here. Ones no one knew about—since his grandmother would throw a fit, and his brothers would want to know details he couldn't give them. But his time with North Star hadn't been a waste—and not just because Ace was in jail.

Cody turned toward the sound of an engine. A police cruiser stopped on the gravel. His eldest brother stepped out, hat shielding his face from the sun and Cody as he walked toward him.

"Jamison." It was strange. He'd spent most of the past few years staying away from the family and focusing on North Star and bringing down the Sons. When he'd crossed paths with Jamison last month, it had been as an agent.

The past few weeks when Jamison had come home had thrust him back into the role of baby brother. It had grated.

Until this moment, when Cody felt something like relief wash through him. Because here was someone who would know what to do. Not about the case, but about this horrible feeling inside of him he couldn't seem to control.

Jamison studied him, as if he could understand everything just from a look. "So."

"I have a daughter." It was such a stupid, pointless thing to say since Jamison surely knew, and yet Cody hadn't really said it out loud like that yet. Somehow, his oldest brother brought that out of him.

"So I hear. Hell of a thing."

"Yeah."

"Liza tells me Nina's recovering."

Cody nodded.

"Look, um…" Jamison cleared his throat and slid off his hat, rubbing the back of his neck. "I have some inkling of what you're feeling right now."

"Liza didn't show up with your kid in tow."

"No. She didn't," Jamison agreed easily. "But there was baggage. And I thought, well, we'd deal with the threat and Ace, and then I could figure that all out. It isn't going to work that way. I think, especially with a kid in tow."

"She calls me Daddy."

Jamison made a pained expression as if he understood. Pain and joy and a million conflicting emotions. How could Cody do anything but put them away until he'd secured his daughter's safety?

"I think you should go see Ace."

Cody could only stare for a full thirty seconds at his brother. Age had etched lines onto his face, but it was the same face it had always been—a little harder, a lot more determined and holding far more responsibility than any one man could contain.

Except Jamison had always managed.

"I don't think me seeing Ace right now would be a good idea."

"I know. But you held yourself back that day. You didn't end his life and you could have."

Should have.

"If you see him, talk to him, we might be able to

get a handle on what he knows about what happened to Nina," Jamison said in his rational, cop voice.

"I can't right now, Jamison. I can't..." It burned to admit a weakness. "I don't have the control I need."

"Okay. What if we send Nina?"

Chapter Six

Nina sat in the living room of the Wyatt house with Liza, Brianna and Gigi playing with plastic ponies on the rug. Grandma Pauline and Dev had gone out to do ranch chores, and Duke had returned to his neighboring ranch.

Not before he and Grandma Pauline had fought over where she and Brianna should stay. But Grandma Pauline had the trump card: six grandsons who were all law enforcement or had been. Duke had Sarah and Rachel living at home—who no one wanted to bring into this mess.

Which brought home the fact she hadn't seen any of her sisters. Duke and Liza were the only ones from her life with the Knights who'd come to see her.

Nina shouldn't be surprised, and she had no right to feel hurt, but she was both and a little miserable with it. That and the aching pain in her stomach. She knew she could take more pain medication, but she'd deal with the pain over the loopy exhaustion that consumed her as a side effect from the meds.

"You can always go lie down," Liza offered gently.

"No. I'm tired of lying. I'm really tired of thinking." She picked at the arm of the couch. "I haven't seen any of the other girls."

Liza winced. "Well, Cecilia's had to work. And Felicity too, of course. They don't live at the ranch."

"But Rachel and Sarah do."

"I'm sure Rachel will come around. Sarah… Truth be told, she's not exactly sold on *me* being back yet, and I've been here two months. We may have had our reasons for leaving, Nina, but…"

"I know." Aside from Rachel, who was Duke and Eva's only biological child, they'd all grown up in varyingly tragic circumstances before being taken in by the Knights. They each had their own childhood scars. Being abandoned by the sisters they'd learned to love would be a particularly difficult blow.

"I had to, Liza."

"I don't doubt it." Liza smiled sadly. "The problem with doing things we have to do is that sometimes no one else can understand that need." Liza looked down at their two girls—because even if Gigi was Liza's half sister, she was a little girl Liza was taking care of. "It's really hard to understand when you don't have this kind of responsibility. So, they're struggling, but I understand you did what you had to, Nina. Really."

Nina nodded. She knew Liza was right. As much as she appreciated Liza saying she understood, it didn't assuage all those other things she felt at her sisters not coming to see her. Maybe she should go lie down as Liza had suggested.

But she heard the back door slam and low voices in

the kitchen. A few moments later, Cody and Jamison strode into the living room.

Nina thought Cody's mood might have calmed some before he returned. But there was absolutely no change in all that angry energy that swirled around him.

Nina smiled at Jamison. It was such a strange parade of so many people she'd loved and had had to ruthlessly cut out of her life. She didn't know how to cope with it all.

The years were on Jamison's face. Or maybe it was all the responsibility he hefted on his shoulders that made him look so hard. So much older.

Everything about that hard face softened as Gigi squealed and ran over to him. He lifted her into his arms, and it was clear that Liza's half sister adored him. And that he adored her.

"Missed you, mite," he said in a low tone as Gigi snuggled into him.

Even back when Nina had been desperately in love with Cody, so sure they'd spend their lives together, children had never been a part of her future plans. No matter how much Duke and Eva had loved her, she'd lived under the specter of her parents' choices. She'd been determined to choose the opposite of all of them.

As much as Brianna had become the center of her whole life, sitting in the Wyatt house, her daughter on the floor, Jamison holding a little girl... It didn't feel real.

But Jamison spoke, and it was in that same calm, comfortingly in-control tone she remembered. "Hi, Nina. How are you feeling?"

"I'm all right." She was dead exhausted, but there was so much going on. So much to think about.

Jamison and Liza shared a glance that had Liza getting to her feet. "Hey, girlies, what about if we go visit the horses?"

Brianna jumped to her feet. "Can we feed them?"

"Well, we'll have to ask Uncle Dev."

Jamison handed Gigi off to Liza, and they exchanged a brief kiss, like some kind of perfect choreographed dance that made Nina's chest ache and her eyes search for Cody.

He was looking at the floor.

"You girls go get your shoes on," Liza urged, shooing them toward the kitchen.

"Are we sure it's safe for Brianna to run around outside?" Nina fretted.

"It's safe," Cody said, his voice hard and final. But that eased her nerves some. Cody wouldn't promise safety where there was none.

"What's going on?" Liza demanded of Jamison.

"We're just going to talk to Nina," Jamison replied.

Liza folded her arms over her chest. "About what?"

Nina had to smile at the warning and protectiveness in Liza's tone. Maybe Sarah was still getting over the betrayal of her leaving, maybe all the girls were, but Liza understood. Someone really understood and wanted to protect her. That was nice.

Jamison turned to Nina. "How would you feel about going to visit Ace in jail?"

Nina's gaze immediately flew to Cody's, but aside

from a set jaw and the same furious eyes, she couldn't read his feelings.

She supposed his feelings didn't matter. "What would be the purpose?"

"To see if he has a reaction. To see if he gives anything away."

"Ace isn't stupid," Liza scoffed.

"No, but he's beyond arrogant. He certainly gave some things away when he had us that he shouldn't have."

"He *had* you?" Nina demanded, her gaze whipping to Liza.

Liza shrugged. "I had to get Gigi out from under the Sons, and Jamison helped. Then Cody rescued us."

"It wasn't me," Cody said gruffly.

Liza rolled her eyes. "I'll take the girls out, but don't agree to anything you don't want to do, Nina. Don't let these two push you around." She moved onto her toes and brushed a kiss against Jamison's cheek. "And you don't be pushy."

She walked out into the kitchen, and Nina noted that Jamison and Cody both waited to speak until the sounds of little girls' voices faded and the door closed.

"It's completely up to you, Nina," Jamison offered into the silence. "The problem we're running into is we're not quite sure why the Sons targeted you so violently after such a long time of not."

"It's possible they just couldn't find me."

"In Dyner?" Jamison replied with a raised eyebrow.

"It's possible."

"It's possible," he finally agreed. "But the man shot

you. Maybe he was acting out of turn, but I doubt it. Not if he led with shooting. There's something more to this than just wanting to hurt you because you dated Cody once upon a time."

"Brianna?" she asked, fear icing her insides.

Jamison shook his head. "There's nothing to point to the Sons or Ace knowing about Brianna."

Cody still hadn't spoken, which poked at her irritation. "Don't you have anything to say?" she demanded.

He met her gaze, but only shook his head.

She wanted to punch him.

"I wouldn't," he said, his voice low and lethal against the dead quiet of the room.

Nina realized she'd curled her hands into fists and her thoughts on his behavior had been written all over her face. She lifted her chin and slowly released her fingers. She looked at Jamison and tried to come up with a bland expression.

"So what would you have me do?"

"We'd arrange for you to visit Ace. I'd be with you. We'd let Ace lead the conversation. See if he makes threats or shows his cards about what he does know. He'll try to get in your head, make you afraid, but that might give us some answers. Or some clues to follow."

"And if he gives you clues?"

"We see if we can connect him to your shooting and add it to the charges against him. We also find out how he's controlling things from the inside. Ideally."

"And if things go less than ideally, we go in there and get nothing."

"It's possible. Liza's right. Ace isn't stupid. He's

spent a lot of time evading just what he's facing now. But he's facing it, because of Cody."

"It wasn't just me," Cody insisted again.

Jamison glanced at Cody. "But he'll put the blame square on you."

Something passed between the brothers that Nina couldn't read, which was irritating enough. But Cody just standing on the sidelines while Jamison handled all this irritated her even more.

"So, it's a test of sorts."

"Yes, a test where the risk is minimal. I don't think there's a chance this doesn't connect to the Sons, which means there isn't a chance Ace doesn't know exactly who you are. I know you won't bring up Brianna, and neither will I. We're not trying to find out if he knows Brianna exists. We're just going to see if he'll let anything slip. If he doesn't, we're in the same exact place we are right now."

Nina nodded. She didn't want to face Ace again. The last time had been scary enough. And clearly neither Cody nor Jamison knew that Ace had been the one to come to her to make sure she broke things off with Cody and disappeared.

She should probably tell them, but the words wouldn't form. If Cody could stand there being stoic and silent, she would find a way to be the same.

"I'll do it," she offered, lifting her chin and fighting away the nerves that already threatened. "On one condition." She turned her gaze to Cody. "I don't want Jamison to come with me. I want you to."

CODY HAD SPENT a lot of time learning how to control his reactions. You didn't get to be part of North Star if you were a hothead who couldn't manage his temper. And there'd been a lot of tests to make sure Cody could handle taking down the Sons when it was personal for him.

He didn't understand why Nina broke all those pieces of control he'd honed for so long. He tried to convince himself it was just about being kept in the dark about his daughter's life for six years—but there was an annoying part of himself that knew it was more than that.

It was just her.

Whatever they'd been in their adolescence, it hadn't been ordinary. It hadn't left him. It had marked him, and for a man who had an evil gang leader of a father, nothing so simple and ordinary should mark him.

But she had.

Cody knew Jamison was waiting for him to answer. He knew Jamison would back him up whatever he said—but that only made the decision worse. He had to make the right one, not the one he wanted to make.

"All right then," he said, against his will, against his better judgment. He already didn't want Nina talking to Ace. It would be worse if he was there.

It was also a necessary step. They couldn't just hide out here forever. Brianna would need to go to school. She deserved a normal life. Something had to be figured out and there was no doubt in Cody's mind that Ace was the key.

"I'll make the arrangements then," Jamison said

with a nod. He glanced at Nina then back at Cody. "I'll just go see what the girls are up to."

Code for *leave you two alone to talk this out*.

There was no way to talk it out. No way to make this work. There was only the slog of doing, but there was no point in explaining that to Jamison.

"Did he come all this way just to ask me that?" Nina asked after Jamison left. She sounded as exhausted as she looked. He bit back the urge to tell her to go lie down.

"I assume he came all this way because Liza and Gigi are here and he's used to having them underfoot in Bonesteel."

Her mouth curved. "They're so sweet together, the three of them."

Cody could only grunt. It was a strange thing to see his brother, and Liza for that matter, be so domestic. They didn't seem suited for it at all, and yet they seemed happier than he'd ever seen either of them.

Maybe it was just because Ace was in jail, and Liza's dangerous father was dead, but Cody had the uncomfortable feeling it was about things far more *personal* than all that.

He forced himself to look at Nina and focus on the task at hand. But all he could think was he'd created a child with this woman, and the uncomfortable truth he'd admit to no one was that he hadn't exactly been with anyone else.

He'd been recruited by North Star, and that had left him in dangerous situation after dangerous situation. There'd been some flirtation with Shay, but they'd both taken their positions in North Star too seriously to risk their jobs by acting on said flirtation.

So.

"There are some things I should tell you before we see Ace."

If there'd been any warm and fuzzy memories threatening for purchase, those words doused them in ice-cold water.

Nina clasped her hands in front of her, sitting in the armchair where Grandma Pauline did her crocheting. Nina's complexion was near gray and what she really needed was rest.

"It'll take Jamison some time to set up a meeting. We have time to go over a game plan. You're not looking so hot. I didn't break you out of the hospital so you could run yourself ragged and have to go back."

She stared at him, eyebrows drawing together. "You've changed," she said as if it came as some surprise.

"You're damn right."

"At first I thought it was just because of Brianna, but it's not. Is it?"

Brianna had changed him. Just her existence shifted something inside of him. He didn't know quite what yet, or what to do about it, but being a father—missing six years of that fatherhood—it meant things were different now.

If only he could get a handle on it all.

"You were never sweet, Cody. But your certainty and your plans weren't built on anger."

He kept his gaze stoic, but his words were more caustic than he'd wanted. "Weren't they?"

"Okay, maybe they were." She seemed to mull that over. "But you had more in you than anger."

And what had happened? Nina had broken up with him. She'd been the one bright spot. Ace had almost killed Dev, and his brothers had been determined to back away from Ace. Let him wreak his havoc as long as it wasn't on them.

Cody had been left with no anchor if it wasn't trying to end Ace—if it wasn't having that shared goal with his brothers. So, he'd had Nina, and then she'd left. And he'd known it was because of who he was. Who he came from.

What was left when his shared purpose with his brothers had been taken from him and she'd left him? Nothing but work, and work was bringing down the father who'd made him. So it was all anger. For more years than he cared to count.

But it seemed Nina couldn't let him even come to grips with all that before dropping another one of her many disastrous bombs.

"He came to see me. Ace did. Back then."

Chapter Seven

Nina knew she needed to say more, but her throat seemed to close up. There was a trickle of fear in admitting it to Cody—in seeing the way his eyes flashed with a new somehow brighter fury than he'd been carrying around for days.

"What did you say?" he asked, his voice as dangerous as a blade.

"When you were doing your CIA internship," Nina managed to choke out. "I was going to classes at the community college and living in a little apartment in Sioux Falls. I worked at a coffee shop and…" She felt a wave of dizziness wash over her and knew she should have taken his or Liza's suggestion to lie down seriously.

Everything hurt and now she felt nauseous with it, but she could hardly stop. "Ace walked in. Like he was any other customer. I only knew him because of the pictures you'd showed me of him." Before that moment, she'd thought it sweet, if a little unnecessary, that Cody insisted she knew what Ace looked like and made sure she hid if she ever saw him.

Then he'd walked into that coffee shop and she'd known Cody had been right all along. She'd frozen, not run away like Cody had always told her to. Ace's gaze had landed on her and Nina had known a true fear she hadn't had since she'd been a little girl unable to wake up her unconscious parents.

It had been worse somehow in that coffee shop because she thought she'd been safe and happy up until that moment. At home, her first home, fear was all she'd ever known.

And suddenly it had come back.

"I was the only one behind the counter, so I couldn't run away like you'd always told me to. He ordered coffee and a scone." She could still see it all in her mind's eye, like a movie.

Ace had smiled at her, treated her like any other customer might. Still she'd known. And the more he'd acted normal—paid his tab, sat down at a table and pretended to enjoy his scone and the scenery—the more she'd turned into a jumpy, scared mess.

"He didn't do anything. Just ordered and ate and left, but when I went out to my car after my shift ended, there he was."

Nina left out the detail where he'd been holding a knife. Not threateningly exactly. He'd played with it, but Nina had known it was a threat no matter how out in the open they were.

"It was still light out, though not by much. People came and went. No one… I guess I could have run away or yelled, but he didn't do anything. He just talked."

It seems my youngest son has a soft spot for you, Nina Oaks—for you and the law. I don't plan on allowing him any vulnerability.

"And what did he say?" Cody asked. She knew him well enough, even seven years later, to realize he was trying to sound tough and unaffected while he was anything but.

Nina paused. It was so long ago he hardly needed *all* the details. "Nothing much. It wasn't threatening so much as a warning. He didn't want you distracted, he said. He pretended to be a concerned father. I knew he wasn't, and he made sure I knew that whatever he *said*, his true intent was to threaten me into staying away from you."

"That was why you broke up with me." He lifted a negligent shoulder. "So?"

"No, that isn't why I broke up with you, Cody." She wouldn't let it hurt that he'd think she was so weak as to have a threat work on her. She'd been too stupid at the time—too sure Cody would handle it.

Until…

He gave her a disbelieving look, which didn't surprise Nina in the least.

"I went back to my apartment and started packing just like he told me to. I thought I could get home or at least to Bonesteel. If I could get to your brothers, I knew they'd help me out and I thought… I had it in my head once you heard, you'd come home."

"I would have."

Nina nodded. "I know. So I was packing up all my stuff and I realized when I started throwing my toiletries in a bag that I hadn't… Well, that I might be pregnant."

"Why did that change anything?"

Everything. "I had to stop thinking about myself and what I wanted and focus instead on what my own child would need."

"You decided *my* own child didn't need me," he said, his control slipping bit by bit. "*You* decided that you'd protect her on your own," he said, pointing a finger at her. "*You* made those decisions and what do you want me to say *now*? What do you want me to feel?"

She shook her head, tears filling her eyes. "I don't know. I can't… I just wish you could understand that I didn't want to. I loved you more than anything. I just didn't see a way she could be safe if anyone with the last name Wyatt knew she existed."

"I would have protected her. Why is it different? You thought I'd come home if I knew my father had threatened you, but you didn't think I'd do everything in my power to keep my own child safe?"

"What did he care about me, Cody? I was a nobody, doing nothing special. But he threatened me. Just because you loved me. What would he do to a child who was half yours? Part his?"

"Brianna is nothing of his," Cody replied so viciously she flinched.

"To us," Nina managed to return though she was starting to shake. "To her. But to Ace? He'd consider her his."

"If I'd known any of this, I would have killed him when I had the chance."

Her heart twisted. He believed that, but she knew it wasn't true. Whatever had happened, whatever little she knew about it, she knew Cody wouldn't, maybe *couldn't* kill in cold blood. To protect someone he loved? Sure. But not just to end something.

A tear slipped over her cheek, but she had to get this out. She didn't think they could ever get on the same page—for Brianna—if they didn't really get this out. Maybe he'd never understand, but it had to be out in the open.

"If you'd known, you would have wound up dead before Brianna was even born." She hadn't wanted to tell him this part of it. It was cowardly, she knew, but she wanted to protect her heart—the one that had never stopped loving him. "I don't think you understand I was trying to protect *you* as much as her."

His face went slack a moment before he pulled himself back together, as if he sucked in all those emotions and shoved them behind a blank facade. Locked them up and hid them away—far away from her.

"Go take a nap, Nina. I'll let you know when I have the details for the meeting."

Then he walked away. Again.

And she was too tired to go after him.

CODY WORKED HIMSELF to the bone on ranch chores the rest of the day. He checked in with Shay but only reached her voice mail. He tested all his security—that no one on the ranch knew he'd set up.

Grandma believed Ace wouldn't step foot on the ranch because of some curse she'd put on him back when her daughter had still been alive and not totally convinced of Ace's evil. Cody's belief in curses didn't extend far enough to think his father could be scared by one.

So, years ago, on a variety of visits, he'd slowly begun installing a complicated and extensive network of security measures around the entire property.

He'd never even told Jamison about it. He supposed he should now. It was the day for telling people things.

He'd never tell Grandma. She'd skin him alive. Once upon a time he'd thought her invincible, but these days, whether it be her age or his, he understood all too well she was also a target. Maybe Ace did believe in her curse, since he fancied himself something of a god, but that only meant he'd find a way to make Pauline pay.

Because Ace Wyatt was determined to make every one of his sons pay for the betrayal of leaving, the insult of going into law enforcement, which he thought was the lowest occupation known to man.

You didn't cross Ace.

Worst of all, Ace had the patience to make you wait years, or even decades, before he decided it was time for retribution.

Cody kept thinking about the day he'd saved Jamison and Liza from Ace's clutches. He'd had a gun, held it to Ace's head. He could have pulled the trigger. He could have ended everything.

But all he'd been able to think in the moment, thanks to Jamison, was that'd only make him like Ace.

Sometimes Cody feared it was in his DNA, in his

bones, to be too hard. To be cruel. To be evil. Maybe it was.

But he chose, time and time again, not to give in to it.

Cody stood outside, looking up at a starry sky, freezing and yet not being able to bring himself to go inside. Because if he continued that choice of good over evil, he had to find a way to handle Nina. To be kind. To find some form of understanding.

He just kept playing the conversation over and over in his head. The way she'd cried. The way she'd clearly left some things out to spare his feelings.

This terrible thing inside of him wondered if she was right. If she'd told him about being pregnant and being threatened by Ace, he would have gone off half-cocked and probably gotten himself killed.

Had she really made the right choice? He supposed they'd never know. Cody had to live with that decision either way.

He blew out a breath and slipped inside. He heard Grandma and Dev talking in low tones in the kitchen and bypassed it, instead heading upstairs. The bedroom Nina was staying in had the door closed with no light coming from underneath it.

He inched down the hall toward voices. When he looked into the open door to the room Brianna and Gigi were sharing, he found Liza on one of the small beds—a girl on either side of her. She was reading a story complete with dramatic theatrics, and the girls were eating it up.

When she finished the book and looked up, she

smiled at Cody. "It's getting late, girlies. Come on, Gigi. Let's go brush your teeth."

Gigi grumbled, but she got out of her bed and followed Liza out into the hall. Cody smiled weakly at Brianna, who looked so small with her hair wet and her pink sparkly pajamas.

"Maybe you'd let me read it to you?"

Brianna smiled brightly at him, holding up a book. "Will you do the voices?"

"Uh… Sure. I guess. I can't promise I'll be as good as Liza."

"Even Mom isn't," she said in a conspiratorial whisper.

Cody couldn't help but smile at that. Gingerly, he slid onto the bed next to her. He took the book she handed him and began to read. He felt foolish, but he tried to do voices for the dragon and the princess. The more Brianna laughed, the easier it was to get into it.

When he finished the story, Brianna was snuggled into his side. "I'm glad we're here," she said.

Cody gave her a gentle squeeze. "Me too."

"Did you know when Liza and Jamison get married that Gigi will be my aunt?" she laughed, then looked up at him as her expression sobered. "Can we all live together now? Forever? Uncle Dev is going to teach me how to ride horses."

Cody didn't know how to answer the question. Not by a long shot. "I can teach you to ride horses."

"Really? Uncle Dev said you're not very good."

"Uncle Dev is full of sh— Full of…it." *Uncle Dev.* This was his life. And weirdly this life he'd never planned to have—the ranch and living under his grandmother's roof—was exactly the life he wanted to give her.

"I don't know what's going to happen yet, Brianna. The one thing I know is I'm going to keep you safe, no matter what. Whether I'm with you or not, I want you to know I'm doing everything I can to keep you safe. I promise you that, and I do not break my promises."

"The bad men are coming again," Brianna said, looking down at her book.

Cody noted it wasn't a question, and there was a weary resignation to her voice. Too resigned for a girl of six.

But he'd been, hadn't he? He'd known exactly the kind of danger his life held for him at this age. He should keep her here, resigned and weary so she didn't get any ideas. So she didn't make any mistakes.

He couldn't bear it. "What did your mom tell you about the Wyatt brothers?"

Brianna lifted her face, mouth curving just a hint reminding him so much of Nina's smile he almost couldn't breathe. He'd loved Nina more truly and fiercely than he'd ever imagined possible, and no matter how the years passed he couldn't convince himself it had been an illusion or even teenage idiocy.

"She always told me stories that you all were brave knights."

Cody nodded. "And brave knights always win, Brianna. In the end, good wins."

He hadn't always believed that, but now that he had a daughter, he had to. For her.

Chapter Eight

It was happening too fast. Nina had hoped to have weeks before she'd have to confront Ace. But Cody had tersely informed her they'd be going to speak with Ace tomorrow.

That had thrown her for a loop this morning, made her edgy and irritable. Even more so when no one would let her do anything. Grandma Pauline insisted she sit whenever she walked into the kitchen. Liza shooed her away from the laundry. Even Brianna wouldn't play with her, telling her to lie down—she was going to feed the chickens with Gigi and Grandma Pauline after breakfast.

So Nina wandered the house achy and irritable. When she heard low male voices, she moved toward the kitchen.

The Wyatt brothers sat around the kitchen table. They made quite a sight together. Tall, broad men— Gage was in his uniform, Tucker had a gun holster strapped to his chest. Dev was in ranch clothes, Brady and Jamison in plainclothes, as was Cody. They all looked incredibly grave.

"She'll have to have a script of some kind," Tucker was saying, spreading his hands out on the table. "We have to be careful and meticulous."

Gage shook his head. "A script would be too obvious. She'd sound stilted and Ace would smell a rat."

"He can't smell a damn thing past his ego," Dev muttered irritably.

Nina stood in the entrance to the kitchen and blinked. They were making plans. About her. *Without* her.

"What is this?" she demanded.

No one responded. Cody lifted a hand and offered a dismissive wave.

She wasn't sure she'd ever wanted to punch someone as much as she did in that moment.

"If we don't go the script route, then we should practice," Tucker was saying, looking around the table to meet each of his brothers' gazes.

But not Nina's.

"What? Like role-play?" Gage returned with a snort.

"It's an effective training tool," Cody retorted, clearly unamused. "Practicing what you're going to say can give you a confidence. It can prepare you for the different ways a conversation can go."

"Nothing's going to prepare anyone for Ace," Dev said gruffly.

"I *have* faced Ace before," Nina noted.

"He's going to eat her up and spit her out and give us nothing," Dev continued bitterly without even glancing at Nina.

"I am right *here*."

Gage smiled up at her. "Of course you are, darling."

He didn't seem to register the killing look she sent him. So she did the only thing she could think to do.

She walked over to Grandma Pauline's dinner bell, which she knew didn't get used too often anymore. Never with a tableful of people already sitting down. She grabbed the wooden spoon off the hook—as this wooden spoon was specifically meant for striking the bell for stubborn, hardheaded men.

She struck the spoon against the bell as hard as she could.

It echoed and clanged and all six men flinched and looked in her direction.

"Is that all it takes to get your attention then?" she asked sweetly.

"We don't have much time to plan," Cody said.

"No, *we* don't. As I'm the main player in this little act, shouldn't I have a seat at this table? Or am I too feeble to handle the particulars of what *you* are asking *me* to do?"

All six men shifted uncomfortably. They looked at Jamison as if to say *you handle her*. She stared him down, slapping the spoon against her palm just like Grandma Pauline did when she was waiting for an explanation of poor behavior.

"He's our father," Jamison replied calmly, though he eyed the spoon suspiciously. "We know him as best as he can be known. It should be our plan, Nina."

"But I'm the one who has to put the plan in play, which means I deserve a spot at the table."

Both Jamison and Cody's mouths firmed, but Tucker

stood. "She's right, of course." He smiled and motioned for her to take his seat.

She didn't smile at him, since it felt all too placating, but she took the seat because she deserved it.

Then they all looked at her expectantly and she realized she hadn't thought *this* part through. She'd just been mad that they weren't including her. She didn't actually have any ideas.

"So?" Cody asked, and she didn't miss the edge of irritation in his voice.

She smiled sarcastically at him, brain scrambling for something intelligent to say. She made a big show of clasping her hands together in front of her on the table and cleared her throat. "Well. I haven't heard everything you six have cooked up without me. Why don't you fill me in on how far you are first?"

"We haven't gotten anywhere," Gage said, and he was grinning at Cody like he was amused at his brother's clear irritation. "We've argued."

"How like you all," Nina returned. Which earned her a chuckle from Gage and no one else.

"We need a game plan," Cody said sourly. "We're trying to agree on one."

"Before you plan any games, which this isn't, you need to start with the goal."

"The goal is to get Ace to talk, without realizing he's given us anything," Jamison said.

Nina nodded. "We're trying to figure out what he knows. Which means the first step is giving him a darn good reason I'm going to see him. He shouldn't think we're trying to get information. He should think we're trying to prove something. If *I'm* coming to see him out of nowhere, it has to be solid."

"He shot you. Isn't that enough?" Dev replied.

Nina shook her head and noticed Cody was doing the same. Well, at least they were on the same page with some things. "*He* didn't shoot me. In fact, I killed the man who did. Right?" She looked at Tucker for confirmation even though she had no doubts. But he was the detective on the case.

Funny how life worked.

"There was a dead body in what remained of the house, yes."

Nina nodded, making sure she held the gaze of every man at this table. She'd learned something in seven years—you never got to show you were afraid. If you did, people took advantage. The Wyatt brothers might think they'd never take advantage of her, but this was about bringing their father down. She was only a pawn. A piece.

She wouldn't let them walk all over her when she had her own wrongs to right.

"We need more than the attack. We need something…something that feels like revenge."

"Well, there's the obvious," Brady said, speaking for the first time.

Cody frowned at his brother. "What's the obvious?"

"Seven years ago Ace warned you off, right?" Brady said to Nina. "Didn't want you seeing our boy here. Then, for whatever reason, seven years after you disappear, he—or someone in the Sons—targets you."

Gage nodded, though Nina didn't understand at all

what they were getting at. She glanced at Cody, whose face had gone hard.

"What? What's so obvious that I'm missing?"

Gage and Brady looked pointedly at Cody. He sighed heavily. "We go there to prove something to Ace." He didn't move—not one inch. She wasn't even sure he breathed he was so still, but there was a shift in the air around him. Around them. "That he didn't succeed—either time."

For a few moments, Nina could only stare. Then she could only laugh, though it hurt her stomach something awful. "You're..." She laughed some more, unable to stop. Made worse by the fact the Wyatt brothers looked at each other in some mix of confusion and unease.

It took her a few minutes to really get ahold of herself enough to speak. "You expect Cody to be able to go in there and convince anyone that he's shooting daggers at me because we've reconciled?" She shook her head. "I don't think anyone's that good of an actor, let alone him."

"You'd be surprised what I can pretend when my daughter's life is at stake."

"Except that cold, disgusted way that you say that proves otherwise, Cody." And it hurt, no matter how she wished it didn't.

"Why don't we leave you two alone and—"

"You will not move," Nina snapped. "We will finish this before Brianna comes back inside. She understands more than I'd ever want her to, but she doesn't need the details. Cody, you think you can pretend we've somehow found a way to reconcile, then that should be the road we take." She wouldn't let herself crumble just because her feelings were a little hurt. "We're there to rub it in his face. Maybe even act like we're thanking him for bringing us back together. The more smug we are, the more likely he'll be to want to burst our bubble. It's the best chance to get him to slip up and give us a clue."

No one spoke or reacted for a few seconds. So she looked at Jamison. He was their leader, no matter that the younger ones might not admit it. They all looked to Jamison for the final decisions because once upon a time he'd saved all his brothers from hell while he'd been stuck there himself.

Eventually, he nodded. "It's a good plan."

"You should practice," Gage offered, and though he was trying to hold back a smile, Nina didn't miss that he found the whole thing *humorous*.

She scowled at him.

"Have, if not a script, an idea of how you're going to lead the conversation," Tucker said, with a little more tact than his brother. "Practicing will help make it seem natural."

Cody smiled, a complete and utter fake smile Nina didn't buy for a moment. "Goody."

THE BROTHERS WENT their separate ways, leaving Cody alone with Nina in the kitchen. Which was the last place he wanted to be right now.

"You should rest." She didn't look as pale as she had yesterday, but she certainly wasn't 100 percent. She'd been shot. Gone through surgery and been bro-

ken out of the hospital far too soon. "You should let
Brady check you out."

"We should..." She wrinkled her nose. "Practice
isn't the word I'd use. We should plan."

"Brianna and Gigi will be back any minute. There's
no use practicing if you're only going to keel over because you aren't taking care of yourself."

She made a snorting sound. "Trust me, Cody, if
there's one thing I know how to do it's take care of myself. I didn't have anyone else to do it for me."

"Which sounds like a 'your choice' type deal."

"Yes, my choice. Certainly nothing to do with my
boyfriend's psychotic father."

"Right. Well..." He had nothing pithy or even snippy
to say to that. Nothing at all to say to the truth. He
could be angry. He could mourn the loss of six years,
but he couldn't quite bring himself to believe it wasn't
all necessary.

Because Ace had put a target on his back the day
he'd been born. Cody had just been too old when he
realized it.

"Cody." Her voice sounded so soft, so entreating.
When she slid her hand over his, it was as if the years
fell away. "I don't blame you. Not for Ace. Why would
I?"

Why wouldn't you?

The kitchen door opened, and Brianna clattered in-
side, already halfway through a story about chickens.
She skidded to a stop in between the chairs Nina and
Cody both sat in.

"Grandpa Duke said I could go over to his ranch

and meet all his horses and he has three dogs and two cats and—"

"No." He knew he'd been too harsh when Brianna's face crumpled, but it killed him that she was so excited about something that absolutely could not happen.

He glanced at his grandmother and Liza standing in the door with their arms crossed over their chests in exactly the same way. Then he met Nina's hurt and confused stare.

"We have to stay on the property," Cody said, and no matter how he told himself to be hard, to be strong against that vulnerable cast to her expression, he found himself gentling the words against his will.

"And why's that?" Grandma demanded.

He might have lied if not for the fact Brianna was looking up at him with big blue eyes as if the world rested on his next words.

"I have safety precautions here. I'll know if someone's coming. Here. I don't know about Duke's property." He pulled Brianna onto his lap so he could be eye level with her. "I am sorry, sweetheart, but we've got to stay here for the time being."

"I like it here. I love it here. It's the best place we've ever lived." She threw her arms around his neck, squeezing tight as her voice wavered. "We can stay here forever. I don't have to go anywhere. Please don't make us. I love it here. Right here."

He flicked a glance at Nina, who looked like she'd been stabbed.

Cody rubbed Brianna's back and tried to find something reassuring to say. "We're good here. Everything's all right," he murmured. She sniffled into his shoulder.

He didn't dare look at Nina or his grandmother. He was sure it would break that last thread of control he had.

"Can I go watch TV?"

"Let's watch Peppa!" Gigi announced enthusiastically.

Brianna sighed heavily, muttering about baby shows, but she slid out of Cody's lap and took Gigi's hand. They disappeared into the living room, and all Cody could do was stare at his empty lap.

"We'll go keep an eye on them," Liza said, looking meaningfully at Grandma.

"Humph," Grandma muttered before following Liza out to the living room.

"Look. I'm sorry. I should have found a better way of… I don't have this…" *Hell*. "I snapped at her and I shouldn't have."

When he looked up at Nina she was barely holding back tears, but she was shaking her head. "It isn't that," she said, her voice squeaky and weak. "I… I didn't realize how miserable she's been."

"She hasn't been—"

"All you said was she couldn't go next door and she begged to be able to stay. She hasn't been happy if she's desperate to stay here."

"Nina…" He didn't know what to say to her. He shouldn't want to comfort her. She'd hidden their child from him. If Brianna was unhappy it *was* Nina's fault.

Except he knew too well what a truly scary childhood looked like. "It isn't something you should blame yourself for."

"When you're in it—deep in it—you don't see. I worried about her safety. I worried about everything, but I didn't spend enough time worrying if I'd given her a childhood."

"Trust me, Nina. Having been the six-year-old who wasn't safe, you had your mind on the right thing. She knows you love her. If she didn't, she wouldn't trust any of us. But she does. Sure, the way she's been raised has left its scars on her, but that happens to everyone. We know better than most how much worse those scars can be."

"You don't have to try and comfort me." She shook her head and stood, wrapping her arms around herself. "I know what I did to you. I know—"

"You don't know everything," he returned, irritated that she was throwing his justified anger in his face. "If my mother had done half of what you've done, my childhood would have looked a lot different, especially at the age of six." Something cold and discordant slithered up his spine, but he pushed it away.

"That's different."

"How?"

"Your father was Ace."

"My father *is* Ace."

"But you aren't. You aren't him. I wasn't saving Brianna from you. I don't know that there was any other way, Cody. I really don't. But it wasn't about you. I just didn't know any other way to keep you both safe. I never… I really never thought you'd believe me."

"I don't want to."

"That's not the same as not actually believing me."

"I don't know about forgiveness, Nina. I don't know how to forgive what I've lost." He didn't know how to do any of this, but Brianna was his. "But I can't blame you, *hate* you for what you did. I don't even think it was wrong. You're probably right. I would've gotten myself killed."

Her jaw dropped and she stared at him like he'd lost his mind.

He probably had. "I *can* admit when someone else is right."

Her mouth curved. "Well, that's new."

He almost—*almost*—laughed. It would have felt good. It would have been nice to laugh with her. But there wasn't much to laugh at here. Tomorrow they'd visit Ace. Nina was in danger no matter who they saw or what they did.

"Jamison was a lot younger than I am now when he was getting me out of the Sons and away from Ace. He had a lot less help too. I would have thought I could do the same, but I wouldn't have thought it through the way Jamison spent our entire childhoods doing. Looking back, I know it wasn't so simple for him. I was the only one he got out before..." That cold, needling feeling was back.

"Before what?"

"When we were seven... Ace considered seven the age of testing. That's when he'd been left and..." It couldn't be. It couldn't... "On my brothers' seventh birthdays he left them each in the middle of the Badlands with no supplies, no nothing. Every birthday you had to spend the amount of days you were old on your own out there. To prove you were worthy of the Wyatt name, to prove you belonged."

"That's awful. How can a seven-year-old be expected to survive on their own?" Nina said, hugging herself tighter.

"They did. They did, but Jamison got me out before..." Cody's gut roiled. "When's Brianna's birthday?"

"What?"

He took Nina by the hands, fear and panic and utter horror beating through him. "When does she turn seven?"

"In three weeks. I—"

He dropped her hands as the icy weight of horror took all the strength out of him. "Ace knows."

Chapter Nine

Nina practically staggered as Cody let her go. She couldn't process his words, but his clear panic had her heart beating so hard in her head she could hardly make out what he was saying.

"I have to get everyone back here. We have to re-formulate." He moved for the door, but never quite finished a movement.

"How does he know, Cody? How is this possible?" It wasn't. It couldn't be. All along, everyone had assured her there was no way Ace had known about Brianna.

"I don't know. Hell. I don't know." He ran a shaky hand through his hair and it was how utterly affected he was that scared her down to her bones. "But it isn't a coincidence. Jamison got me out the day before I turned seven. The timing of Ace coming after you *now* not making sense? It makes a whole hell of a lot of sense now."

"But he didn't know. The man who shot me didn't know Brianna was there. All this time…"

"We don't know what he knew, Nina. You killed him." Cody scraped his hands over his face. "And if the timing… Ace loves his damn timing. The man wasn't meant to take her. He was meant to scare you."

"Why would Ace want to do that?"

"I can't understand everything Ace does, but if there's a why it's usually to screw with you. End of story. I have to stop Jamison before he gets too far. And Tuck. They have to come back and we have to—"

"No. Too many voices. Too many opinions. This is about Brianna, Cody. Which means it's down to us."

"I'm not leaving my brothers out of this. The only reason we ever survived in the first place was—"

"Jamison taking everything upon himself to save the younger ones."

Cody opened his mouth as if to argue, but there was nothing to dispute. She knew the story. You couldn't know the Wyatts and not know how Jamison had slowly and methodically managed to rescue each one of his brothers out of the Sons' camps and gotten them to Grandma Pauline's ranch before finally managing to get himself out, with Liza, when he was almost eighteen and she sixteen.

Nina also knew Cody carried around a certain amount of guilt—she'd always likened it to survivor guilt. He'd been the youngest to get out. He hadn't had to survive what his brothers had to—like this awful seven-year thing.

Nina sank into the chair again. Ace knew about Brianna. "How could he know? Why would he have waited?"

"The reason Ace has done everything he's done is because he has patience. And a plan no one else knows.

He left Dev alive for a reason, Nina. It wasn't out of the goodness of his heart. It wasn't a miracle moment of having a conscience. It was a warning, at best. And I think we all know deep down it wasn't the end. We'd only hoped it was."

She didn't know how to process all this. How to accept that she'd failed. "So, what you're telling me is these six years were a waste. That we could have all been together. It wouldn't have mattered."

He turned to face her, some of that panic or restlessness fading into something a lot closer to shock. "Was that ever what you actually wanted?"

"Of course that's what I wanted. Do you know how… I was so happy, you know, that moment I took that pregnancy test." She could picture it. The gas station bathroom, all her stuff packed up in her car heading back to the Wyatt and Knight ranches. Heading home. "For a brief shining second I thought… I never expected I'd have kids, but I was thrilled. And then I had to deal with reality." Now she had to as well. There was no time for Cody's feelings. There was only protecting their child. "What are we going to say to Ace?"

"If he already knows—"

"We still have to figure out what this is. What he's trying to do."

"I know what it is. It's revenge. It's Ace's sick, twisted view of the world. To him, his sons were property, his celestial reward or whatever. We betrayed him—time and time again. I put him in jail, Nina. Me. So I know what he wants. He wants to hurt me.

And he'll do it in the way he considers himself hurt—through my child."

Nina wouldn't let herself panic, though fear beat through her and threatened to tighten around her throat. She'd been here. She'd faced *this*. "If that's true, all it means is we change our game plan. She's here. She's safe. Nothing has changed."

"Nina." The look of desolation on his face nearly snapped her weakening grip on control.

"I know. Trust me, I know." Her voice wavered so she took a second to firm it. "It feels too big. It feels too…awful, but I have been doing this for six years—with no help. No nothing. I kept her safe."

"Or he let you think that," Cody replied with utter disgust.

As much as she knew that disgust wasn't directed at her, it was too much to bear. Was it true? Had she kept Brianna safe all these years simply because Ace wanted some warped revenge on his own bizarre timeline?

She looked down at her shaking hands, felt the tears trickle down her cheeks. It was almost surreal, how her body reacted when her mind seemed to just go numb.

There wasn't time. She'd been here before—whether Ace had "let" her escape or not, she'd felt in that moment the same as she did now.

Except there was no one to lean on then. She looked up at Cody. He was stricken and close to crying—but he wouldn't. The fear was there, all over his face. A lack of certainty in the way he held himself poised to move but never did.

Neither of them spoke as the horror of Ace knowing

Brianna existed stretched out around them, growing beyond reality into that horrible place she couldn't go.

What if…

What if…

"I can't lose her," Nina managed to say, wiping her wet face with her palms.

"I haven't even had her," Cody said, his voice hoarse and anything but strong.

He was right. He was too right. He hadn't had enough of Brianna. More important, Brianna hadn't had enough of Cody.

Nina couldn't think about how, if Ace truly knew about Brianna's existence, Nina could have had those years of Cody and Brianna together—regardless of what might have happened between *her* and Cody, Brianna would have had her father.

But there was no going back. She'd learned to never finish *what-ifs*. She'd learned to keep going forward. She had learned that once she let the panic out, she had to rein it back in and move forward anyway.

She stood, though a few tears still slipped out, though her legs and arms shook. She crossed to Cody and she took his hands in hers. He'd likely never felt a day of true panic in his life, so she'd have to teach him that parenthood was forever a new panic—and you let it out, and reined it in.

When he met her gaze, she was all too familiar with that particular kind of devastation.

"Maybe Ace knew all along. Maybe that's the only reason Brianna and I survived. But that doesn't mean we couldn't have survived. What it means is Ace gave me six years to practice." She squeezed his hands. "This time, I don't have to do it alone. We have to work together."

ALONE.

It was a strange word to hit him sideways, at an even stranger time. They had so many bigger issues at hand than *alone*.

But that's what he'd been since Nina broke up with him. He'd graduated, gone into North Star and dedicated his twenties to bringing down the Sons and his father. He'd succeeded at neither and he'd kept a good distance between him and his brothers. The people he'd met in North Star had become something like friends, but they hadn't worked together exactly. Everyone had their own specialty. They worked in teams and as a unit, but not for any one reason. Only for one target.

They weren't his brothers. They weren't family.

Now this woman was holding his hand, telling him that teamwork was somehow the answer here. She didn't mean like it had been in North Star. She meant like it had been when he was a kid.

And she was right. He knew she was right because what had saved each of his brothers and himself from the Sons?

Each other.

He would happily go on, singularly trying to keep Brianna safe, but it didn't work. He knew what worked against Ace.

He looked down at Nina, awed, because he never would have realized that if she hadn't reached out to him and said *together*. If she hadn't looked him straight in the eye and *understood* this horrible clutching, all-encompassing fear that left all his normal faculties dimmed.

"Nina." His voice was still rusty, but he forced himself to keep talking without trying to hide it. "Brianna is ours, but this fight isn't. This fight is bigger than her."

"There is nothing bigger than her to me, Cody. Nothing."

Nina tried to pull her hands away, but he gripped them before she could let go. "I understand that. I do. But there is to Ace. Because I am just one of six betrayals. He wants us all to pay. Piece by piece. He wants his symbolic timing and his mind games."

"I don't care what he wants."

"Exactly. You said you're not alone this time—we can win this time. Okay, you don't want to do it alone? Then let's really not do it alone. And I don't just mean my brothers. I mean all of us. Wyatts. Knights. We don't just formulate a plan to keep Brianna safe. We formulate a plan to make her future safe. All our futures safe from him."

"How? How? It's been all these years, Cody, and… he knew. He knew." She shook her head against that truth. "The more people involved the more people get hurt like this."

"Maybe he knew about Brianna. Maybe he'll target her to hurt me. Those things are likely." He had to accept it, like he'd done in North Star when things hadn't gone as planned. You couldn't get emotionally involved. You had to be able to accept failure and move on to the next mission.

But his daughter wasn't a mission and there was no failure he could accept here.

"But I am the reason Ace is in jail. Not because I did anything special, but because Jamison, Liza and I worked together. Now imagine what could happen if you put all fourteen of us together."

"Sixteen," Nina corrected. "Gigi and Brianna are part of this too."

Cody nodded. "Together."

Nina nodded in response. He could see her fears and worries parade across her face, but she nodded. She agreed.

They had a lot of work to do.

"First things first, we need to get everyone here."

"The girls…" Nina trailed off, her expression taking on a new pain. "Sarah and Rachel especially. They don't want to see me."

"When you were in the hospital, and Brianna was bloody and wouldn't speak or let us bathe her, who came over and helped? All of the girls. Brianna trusted them because of your stories. Maybe they don't want to see you, Nina, but they all rallied together to help that little girl. They'll keep doing that. That's what family does."

"I didn't," she said, and everything about how blue her eyes got with tears filling them was heartbreaking and painful.

"You did what you thought was right."

She made a scoffing sound. "Be careful, Cody. That sounds an awful lot like forgiveness."

He heard a peal of laughter from upstairs, Brianna's laughter. Nina had kept him from that for six years, but in this moment he didn't know how to focus on anger. He'd done questionable things to survive Ace, why shouldn't Nina?

"Maybe after this I'll manage to find some. Now. We need to round everyone up."

He instructed Nina to tell Liza the whole story and send Liza over to the Knight ranch to get Duke and inform all the Knight girls. Cody called his brothers who'd left and asked them to turn around. He'd found Grandma and Dev in the barn and brought them up to speed.

It took a few hours to collect them all, but it worked out for the best because it was after Brianna's and Gigi's bedtime. Cody himself had set up a high-tech listening device and camera in the girls' room, though Liza had pointed out drily it was just a baby monitor on steroids.

Grandma had made a big platter of ham sandwiches, an array of sliced fruits and vegetables, and was frosting brownies as they spoke. It had taken Cody twenty-eight years to realize feeding them was how Grandma dealt with stress, fear and worry. He saw it clearly in this moment, with everyone he considered family pressed together around Grandma's kitchen table.

"I think we still need to pay Ace a visit," Cody announced. "We should act like we don't have any suspicions he might know about Brianna."

"Nina isn't going to visit that sociopath," Duke announced.

"Nina will make her own decisions like she has been for the past seven years," Nina replied.

Cody had made her lie down earlier, but he wondered how much she'd slept based on the bags under her eyes. She needed to rest if that bullet wound was ever going to truly heal, but this was hardly a time for resting.

"You can't get anything out of him," Duke said resolutely. "It's a pointless exercise that plays into his hands."

"That isn't exactly true," Jamison countered, a lot more diplomatically than Cody would have. "Ace's biggest flaw is ego. He thinks he's a god of some kind. He believes he knows better than everyone—which is how he's able to be patient and ruthless when it comes to payback."

"For years that man has left you alone." Duke looked at Jamison, then Liza. "If you two hadn't gone interfering—"

"And left Gigi there?" Liza demanded. "Don't play that card, Duke."

Duke shut his mouth and crossed his arms over his chest.

"Personally, I think if Cody and Nina go in acting like they've won, he won't be able to resist telling them how they've lost," Tucker said equitably.

"And in telling us how we've lost, we might just get an idea of what his plan is," Cody continued. "If we don't, we haven't lost anything."

"That you know of," Duke replied darkly.

"It's a risk," Cody returned, holding Duke's angry gaze. "But so is sitting here just hoping he doesn't come after Brianna."

"I say you take that girl and Nina and move to Saskatchewan or some such place and keep them away from danger instead of throwing them headlong into it."

"Brianna deserves her family," Nina said quietly.

"You didn't think that seven years ago," Duke pointed out.

Cody opened his mouth to order Duke to back off, or shut up, or *something*. But Nina shook her head and held up a hand to ward him off.

She looked at Duke, met his gaze head-on. "I was barely twenty-one and had been threatened by the leader of a powerful biker gang. I'd also spent the first eight years of my life in hell, so I figured whatever I gave Brianna would be better than that—especially if it meant everyone else I loved was safe. I can't say I was wrong because I did the only thing I knew how to do in the moment."

She took a deep, shaky breath and let it out. "But I wish I could have given her this sooner. If it's true that Ace knew all along, I could have. Which means he has to pay. And I want to be the person collecting. Not just for my daughter, but for the years he cost me with you."

Silence shrouded the room, a rare feat with fourteen Wyatts and Knights in the same room. Footsteps sounded above, and the monitor crackled with the sounds of movement.

"Let me," Cody murmured as Liza and Nina both stood. "You'll win Duke over better if I'm not here for a few minutes," he whispered to Nina before exiting the kitchen.

He went upstairs and found Brianna standing in the hallway.

"What are you doing up, Brianna?"

She looked up at him solemnly. "Drink of water."

But he could see questions in her eyes. Fear. He crouched to be eye level with her. "Did you hear anything you want to talk about?"

She shook her head, but when she stepped forward and wrapped her arms around his neck he knew there had to be something. Maybe not right now, but she sensed things weren't right. She'd likely overheard *something* over the past few days.

Not to mention she knew her mother had been hurt and her entire life had changed. She had every reason to be frightened no matter how much she liked living at the ranch.

He lifted her as he stood. "Come on. I've got something for you."

"A present?"

"Sort of." He walked to his room, carrying her weight easily—and reveling in how she held on to him. He had a daughter, and she loved him, no questions asked.

He moved into his room and set her on the bed, then went to his dresser, where he'd been keeping what he'd been working on for her. It wasn't perfected, but he had no doubt the necklace would do what he needed it to.

"This is a very special necklace," he said, holding out the piece of jewelry. It was sturdy, made more for purpose than because it was pretty—though he'd tried to give it some pretty touches so she'd want to wear it.

"Is it magic?"

He didn't want her to believe in magic, because some day she wouldn't anymore. But for that same exact reason, he desperately wanted her to believe in possibilities.

"Yeah, I guess it is. But it's emergency magic only. See, if you open it up…" He opened the locket for her and showed her the tiny device he'd attached inside. "See that button?"

She nodded.

"If you push it, I get a notification. It's only for emergencies though. If you're in trouble—real, scary trouble—hit that button and I will come find you."

She chewed on her bottom lip, running her fingers over the edges of the now-closed locket. "Who's Ace?" she asked, keeping her gaze on the necklace.

Cody closed his eyes against the wave of pain. He hadn't expected that question. It was easy to talk about bad men in broad strokes. A little harder when the evil in question came from your own father.

"Ace is a very bad man, Brianna. He wants to hurt us. I know that's scary to hear, and I hate scaring you, baby. But I need you to know he's very bad, and no matter what anyone says, he doesn't ever want to help us."

She finally looked up at him. "Why does he want to hurt me if I don't even know him?"

That question was worse by far. Still, she'd asked it of him—her father—which meant he had to find an answer. "Some people only understand how to be mean. That's why…that's why I—and all your uncles too—became police officers and the like. We wanted to help people instead of hurt them."

She half smiled at him. No surprise since fear and danger were all around them. Even if he'd lied to her and told her nothing was wrong, she would have felt it. She would have known.

He had to hold on to that, and the fact he had a daughter who loved him.

Which meant for the first time he had to go after Ace and also care about what happened to *him*. Because he wouldn't leave Brianna, and he wouldn't lose her.

"I know we haven't known each other that long, but I want you to know I love you, Brianna. More than anything in this world."

She crawled off the bed and wrapped her arms around his neck, snuggling in as he pulled her close and stood.

"I love you too, Daddy." She leaned her head against his shoulder, her whole body relaxing. "I know you'll keep me and Mommy safe."

No matter what.

Chapter Ten

Nina looked at herself in the mirror. No amount of makeup seemed to hide the exhaustion that had marked itself across her face. She was pale, and looked weak.

Maybe that could work in their favor. The point was to make sure Ace underestimated them, because if he did, he would give them something they could work with.

Nina closed her eyes and gripped the sink. She didn't want to take the pain pills for her aching side because they made her too fuzzy, but the over-the-counter painkiller wasn't doing much of anything to take away the dull, throbbing ache.

She breathed, steadily and mindfully, trying to find some peace for a few minutes of meditation.

It didn't work. At all. But she didn't have any more time. She had to face the music.

Not alone though. She'd barely slept all night turning that over in her head. She wouldn't be the scared young girl in a coffee shop parking lot this time. She'd have Cody at her side and the Wyatts and Knights fully behind her.

She was older, wiser, and had people supporting her. And had so much more to lose this time around.

Which was not a particularly meditative thought, so she left the bathroom and headed downstairs. Jamison and Cody were in the kitchen with Grandma Pauline and a furious-looking Duke.

None of the sisters. They'd all come over last night, but none of them had really addressed her. She noted that there was an uneasiness between them and Liza too. Nina and Liza had left and cut ties.

It wouldn't easily be forgiven, but that didn't mean they wouldn't help.

"Ready?" Cody asked, getting to his feet.

Not even close. "Yeah."

It had been decided they wouldn't arrive together. Cody and Nina would drive in one car, trying to give the appearance to anyone who might be watching their moves that they were a happy couple.

Jamison would borrow the Knights' truck and also drive to the jail. Gage would already be there in his cruiser on his shift. Tucker had specifically made an appointment before theirs so that he could be in the jail for investigative reasons in his detective role while Cody and Nina were visiting Ace. Brady and Dev would stay home at the ranch and make sure nothing out of the ordinary was happening on the property while Liza and Grandma watched the girls.

Duke took her by the shoulders. "Just remember, you did this on your own for seven years. You can handle that monster. We'll find a way to destroy him yet."

It was the exact opposite of what he'd said last night,

but that was why Duke had been such an excellent foster father. He might express his opinion, he might loudly disagree, but if anyone was going to go through with whatever he didn't approve of, he turned all that disagreement into support.

She smiled and nodded. He gave her a squeeze, then let her go, and she followed Jamison and Cody out the door to their vehicles.

If the drive felt interminable, she could blame that on nerves and the pain in her stomach. She'd also blame it on Cody's silence and stoic expression.

Even when they finally arrived, Cody said nothing. He led her into the jail, nodding at Jamison in the parking lot, then Gage in the lobby.

When he finally spoke, it was to the woman at the front desk. They filled out the necessary paperwork and were led to various places. Out of nowhere, Cody took her hand and linked it with his.

She stared at it for a moment, surprised by the contact, the warmth and how much that simple gesture steadied her. She wasn't so sure she liked that reminder that she was stupid enough to still be in love with a man who'd never forgive her.

She thought about last night, but shook it away. Cody had been shaken by the realization Ace knew about Brianna. He didn't actually mean anything he'd said about forgiveness.

It would hurt too much to hope for that and not get it, so she had to pretend like it wasn't possible.

They were finally led to a narrow corridor that, unlike the rest of the jail, reminded her of a movie. A small room, rows of cubbies with plastic partitions between this side of the room and the other.

They were led to one of the cubes and told to sit, so they did. After a few minutes of waiting, a door on the other side of the partition opened and Ace was led inside.

He looked exactly like Nina remembered him. Like he hadn't aged, like he hadn't been affected at all by jail.

He smiled as he approached. Nina no longer felt weird holding Cody's hand. It was a lifeline and a reminder Ace couldn't do anything to her in this moment. Because she had Cody.

"Well, son. Isn't this a nice reunion?" His gaze turned to Nina. "What's it been, Nina? Seven years?"

There were many plans in place. They'd gone over them ad nauseum last night. *Pretend they were back together. Pretend Brianna didn't exist. Pretend Cody didn't know anything about why she'd left him in the first place.*

So much *pretending* made her tired, but it was the only option. She shifted her gaze away from Ace and to Cody. Cody withdrew his hand, because he was acting like he didn't know Ace had met with her all those years ago. But also pretending to Ace that he wasn't affected by the pretend bombshell.

God, she wanted a nap. To be far, far away from Ace's dark stare.

"Well, if you were trying to prove to me that you have power even locked in a cell, I'm not very impressed," Cody said. He didn't even sound rehearsed, though they'd all discussed their opening line, edited it until it felt perfect.

Or as flawless as it could be in this situation.

"Do you think everything comes back to you, Cody?" Ace asked, tilting his head and smiling at his youngest son. "That you're singular somehow in my attentions, we'll call them."

Cody only smiled blandly. "I'm the one who put you here, Ace. I almost took your life."

"But you didn't. Because you don't have it in you." He sighed gustily, giving Nina a look that seemed to say *kids these days*. "Which is a shame. The only one of you brave enough to kill me is the only one fit to take my legacy and make it yours."

"None of us want what you have, Ace. No one wants to be a murdering evil psychopath. So you'll have to devise a new plan."

"I haven't killed anyone, Cody. I have no idea what I could have done from here to make you think I'm trying to prove I have power." Ace held up his hands, some attempt to look harmless—honest. *What a crock.* Nina supposed it only failed because they both knew what Ace was so capable of. "But it's so nice to see the two of you together. How did that happen?"

"You tried to kill her. I saved her life."

Nina was amazed at the way Cody could sound smug, when she knew he wasn't. Amazed that he could come off a shade too cocky and sure when she knew he wasn't any of those things in this moment.

Ace's expression went sheepish. "Sorry, son. I've been locked up for weeks now. Perhaps you should see a therapist. I hear they're very helpful in curbing obsessive disorders. You and that little group of yours seem to have *quite* the obsession with me. What were they called? The North Pole?"

"I haven't the faintest idea what you're talking about. But delusions *are* your MO."

"Now this one…" Ace turned his gaze to Nina and smiled again, ignoring Cody's words completely. Nina had to fight the urge to look in the opposite direction from his empty, evil gaze. Ace scared her to her bones, but she had to face him. "Did she ever tell you about our little visit in Sioux Falls?"

"Of course," Cody snapped. Again, Cody's acting amazed her. He appeared both frustrated with the question and vaguely distrusting of her, all while putting on a certain veneer as if he was attempting to fool Ace.

Ace rested his chin on his palms and stared at Nina. Her hands shook, so she shoved them under the table where he couldn't see.

"And what did you tell Cody, sweetheart?"

"I told him w-what happened. That you came to the coffee shop."

"And when I told you to run, you ran. Right?"

Nina looked at Cody. She wasn't nearly as good at acting as he was, but she hoped her true desperation at the situation translated to a despair about what Ace had just said.

"You see, unlike your brothers, Nina has always done what I told her to do. It's why I like her so much. In fact, I downright approve of this little romance."

"You like anyone you can control, Ace," Nina shot

back. Though she still shook, and fear still felt like ice in her gut, it also made her mad. This was the man who'd cheated her out of so much. "But I'm not a little girl anymore."

"No, you're not. Are you? But on the subject of little girls... I suppose we should discuss yours."

"WHAT DOES THAT MEAN?" Cody demanded. Ace wasn't giving him anything he didn't already know, but Ace's MO was also to wait until the person's weakest point. Until everything fell apart. Then strike.

Cody had to fake falling apart, no matter how it galled him to act weak in front of his father. It *was* an act. Nina had told him everything.

He hoped.

"How's Gigi?" Ace asked, changing the subject with an easy grin. "Jamison getting good and bonded with that girl who will come crawling back to the life she was born into once she has a choice?"

"Gigi will never crawl," Cody replied, letting emotion bleed into his voice. His father would see emotion as a weakness, a place to strike. "Least of all to what we saved her from."

Ace's smile made Nina shiver next to him. "Come on. You know everyone comes crawling back to what they know. Everyone." He turned his attention to Nina, studying, calculating.

Cody wanted to jump in front of her. He wished she'd never come. But here she was and they couldn't give away more than they wanted to.

"Sweet, quiet Nina. What *have* you been up to?"

"Nothing," she said a little shrilly. "Nothing except getting shot because of you. I killed your lackey, you know. He's dead."

Ace laughed. "If I knew what you were talking about, and I of course don't, I'd have to make it clear how little I care what happens to any flunky who can't follow directions."

Cody watched his father's expression carefully. Of course it was no outright admission of guilt, but what it did tell Cody was that screwing up was not Ace's plan, as Cody had thought it might have been.

But it made sense the man Nina had killed had failed. Ace had to know how protected the ranch was. He wouldn't have wanted Nina to move there.

Ace's plan had actually backfired. He wasn't quite so powerful from jail as all the Wyatt brothers half believed he could potentially be.

"Must be hard to find good help when your second-in-command gets blown to hell," Cody offered. He tried not to relish the killing, because it would make him too much like Ace, but he felt no guilt for being part of the team that had set explosives that took down Tony Dean and a slew of Ace's other top men in the Sons.

"Yes, isn't it funny how you caused the death of numerous men with your explosives, yet *I* sit in here."

"I find it hilarious," Cody returned, flashing a grin. "Especially when I think about the condition of those twelve girls I saved from the men I blew up. The difference is I can admit that I did it, because the law is on my side, Ace."

"The law." Ace snorted derisively, shifting in his chair. Cody was getting to him. "Morons write laws, and mindless weaklings enforce them. That I raised such spineless, pointless fools is my greatest regret. I was created in the ashes, in abandonment, and I thrived in an unforgiving land devoid of law."

Cody sat back while Ace went off on his tirade about how he built himself from nothing. How their mother had failed them with her inferior genes, and if he'd known he would have killed them all in the womb.

It was downright boring to Cody, slightly satisfying that he'd worked his father up into such a lather. But when he looked at Nina, he watched horror and pain chase over her face. That gave him no pleasure.

"Maybe you can wrap this up in under ten minutes. We do have things to do."

Ace's eyes were manic and bright, but when they landed on Cody that cold chill of foreboding that had preceded a beating in his childhood stole through him. Cody held as still now as he had then.

"When am I going to meet my granddaughter, Cody?"

"Never," he spat.

It was when Ace grinned that Cody knew that momentary high of getting to his father had just cost him getting anything else. Because he couldn't pretend he didn't know about Brianna, or that there was a rift with Nina over it.

Cody stood abruptly. Better to get out than give his father anything else. Better to retreat and let his father think they were weak. "We're done."

"When did she finally tell you? After she got shot? When she had no choice?" Ace made a *tsking* sound. "Your mother tried that on me too. Look where it got her."

Cody all but hauled Nina to her feet and started moving her toward the door. He wouldn't let his father poison her.

"I've watched her all along," Ace called after them. "I have baby pictures, Cody. Do you?"

Nina made a pained noise, so Cody basically pushed her out of the room, following quickly behind. She sagged against the wall, and he wasn't in much better shape himself.

"He won. He did. He got the better of us," she said, sounding close to tears.

"Maybe at the end, but we got what we came for." He had to hold on to that instead of his own idiocy.

"How?"

"We know that he meant to kill you and take Brianna, but the man he sent failed. He failed. You and Brianna have moved to the ranch, which is ten times safer than anywhere else you've been." He took her hands, waited for her to look him in the eye.

The blue of her eyes was vibrant with tears, and it made him feel even weaker himself. When he spoke, his voice was rough.

"You saved her, and yourself. That was no accidental scare tactic. Everything you did that day saved Brianna. If nothing else, you should take some pride in that."

She swallowed. "How can I—"

"Baby, you are the reason you're both alive." Though he shouldn't, though it broke something inside of him he'd been building for probably all these past seven years, he wrapped her in his arms and held her close. "Now I'm going to keep you both safe. No matter what."

Chapter Eleven

The words echoed in her head as Cody went through the rigmarole of getting them back to his car. Nina felt mostly numb.

Everything Ace had said at the end erased any satisfaction in the little piece of information they'd gained. It even erased any pleasure she might have gotten from knowing she'd saved Brianna's life.

Ace had pictures of Brianna. He'd *watched* them. Nina had left everyone she'd loved for nothing.

Nina buckled her seat belt in a painful fog. She didn't dare look at Cody. She'd cry *again*, and she was tired of crying. Tired of hurting—physically and emotionally.

"I know what he said… I know that hurts, Nina," Cody said as he turned on the car. "But he *wants* you to hurt. He's twisting the knife on purpose, and he's an expert."

Cody gripped the wheel, and she could see the tension in him despite how gently he spoke.

"What would have happened? If I hadn't thought

I could keep Brianna a secret from him. What would we have?"

"You can't think like that. Because it didn't happen that way."

Nina looked out the window, desperately blinking back tears. Just because it didn't happen that way didn't mean she didn't ache over those what-ifs.

"I wouldn't have finished my internship," Cody said into the quiet. "I wouldn't have worked for the past six years to dismantle the Sons, which means it's very possible Ace wouldn't be in jail right now. Gigi would still be stuck in the Sons, or worse, dead or trafficked. Liza and Jamison would sure as hell be dead."

"You don't know that."

"Not for sure. But I don't know the opposite to be true either."

"My sisters won't even talk to me."

"They were there last night."

"Because of you."

"Because of you and Brianna. Don't wallow. We don't have time for it."

She scowled at him. "Wallow? I lost seven years of my life I could have given Brianna, and she would have been safe. And happy. Don't wallow? How *dare* you."

"See, if you're ticked off, you're not sad." He smiled at her, and there was a hint of the boy he'd been. A hint of what they'd had.

As much as she'd loved Duke and her sisters, she'd never felt like they fully understood her childhood pain. Looking back now, she realized they probably had, but they'd all been young and self-absorbed and sure in the belief they were unique and alone.

But Cody had always seemed to understand. After all, so much of his childhood had mirrored her own. Negligent, dangerous parents. Fear and death. Then a loving, overwhelming family neither of them could always believe was real.

"I just want to go home," she said on a sigh, closing her eyes and wishing for some kind of respite from all this.

"You mean the ranch."

She shifted uncomfortably. She already thought of it as home. Even though she hadn't lived there growing up, it had been a part of her childhood. She liked Grandma Pauline cooking Brianna breakfast. She loved having the Wyatt brothers as part of the fabric of Brianna's life.

But it wasn't permanent, was it?

"I need ibuprofen, a nap and my daughter."

"Will do."

"Then what?" she asked, a fresh wave of exhaustion bringing back the threat of tears.

"We keep you both safe and see what we can do to figure out how Ace is getting messages to the outside. If we can cut him off completely, then we have nothing to fear."

Nina didn't say what she thought about that, because the truth was she'd always have *something* to fear. Jail wasn't permanent and cutting off ways of getting messages wasn't either. There was no conclusion to this that wasn't temporary.

Except Ace dead.

She thought over what Cody had said—that he'd had a chance and hadn't taken it. She wondered what she would have done in that position. Could she have ended someone's life when it wasn't strictly self-defense?

To protect her daughter from a lifetime of fear... She thought maybe she could.

Would Cody have done something different if he'd known about Brianna?

She pushed those thoughts away, because Cody had one thing right. There was no use wishing things had been different when they weren't. There was no way to change the past. Only ways to survive the future.

She let herself doze, but an odd noise from the car woke her with a start. She glanced at Cody, whose face was grave.

"Don't panic," he said, his voice too deadly calm to be any kind of comfort.

"Don't panic about what?"

"Someone's tampered with the car," he said through gritted teeth. "I need you to call Jamison."

"Cody, I—"

He had a death grip on the steering wheel and she realized that, whatever was wrong with the car, he was fighting to keep it on the road. "Call. Now. Tell him exactly where we are and that someone's following us."

A million questions piled up in her brain, but she understood this was no time for them. She fumbled through her purse and grabbed her phone. She had

Jamison's number programmed in, but when she tried to dial the call failed.

"No service," she said. "I'll keep trying."

"Text instead. It might go through eventually if you try to text. Give him our exact location, say the car has been tampered with, and a white Ford F-150 is following us. I can't make out the plate or the driver." He swore as the car jerked and made an awful grinding noise.

Nina did everything she could to type a clear message, but the car was shuddering now. Her fingers shook no matter how she inwardly scolded herself.

"Whatever you've got, hit Send and hold on."

Nina did as she was told even though she hadn't finished the car description. She hit Send, grabbed on to the arm of her seat.

Then they were flying off the road, and all Nina could do was squeeze her eyes shut and pray.

CODY FELT SOMEONE pulling at him. He heard the faint sound of a woman's voice.

Nina.

His eyes were open, he thought, but he couldn't see anything. Everything was a dim kind of gray. His head throbbed, and he realized the side of his face was wet. He was pretty sure with blood.

He couldn't move his body at first. Couldn't seem to fully find himself in the present moment. He tried to speak, tried to tell Nina he was okay even though it was very much not true.

He'd crashed. That much he could determine. He

took stock of his body. He was still in the car, he was pretty sure. His body hurt, but nothing seemed broken. Except he couldn't see.

"Cody. Cody. Please talk to me."

"I can't see," he finally managed to say, though his voice was raw, and speaking sent a wave of pain through him. He leaned back and away from the air bag that had deployed.

"What?" she breathed. She had to be close. Her voice was soft but audible. He couldn't see. He didn't know where he was. But Nina was talking so she had to be okay, right?

"Are you hurt?" he demanded.

"No."

She was lying. He didn't have to see to hear it in her voice. "Nina."

"Nothing serious. Nothing like… You're covered in blood, Cody. You need help. Serious help."

"I'm fine."

"Cody, you're not looking at me."

There was no point trying to hide it from her. "My eyes are open, aren't they?"

"What do you mean? Of course they're open. Cody, what is wrong?" Hysteria tinged her voice.

"Nina, it's okay. Listen to me. You can't panic, all right?"

"The entire side of your face is covered in blood. And you're *asking me* if your eyes are open. I need to call an ambulance."

"No. No ambulance. I can move. I just can't see exactly."

"Cody. God." She sucked in an audible breath. "You can't see anything?"

He shook his head, winced. "Just gray. Some shadows, but… I can't see. I crashed."

"You crashed." He could hear the way she was fighting against the hysteria, struggling for control. "You won't be able to get out your side. It hit a tree and it's blocked. We'll have to crawl out the passenger side."

"There was a truck following us. Are they coming?" He heard her move though he couldn't see what she was doing.

"I can't see much of anything. Between the air bags and the broken windows. It's hard to say. But we can't move. You have a head injury, and God knows what else. You're not supposed to move."

"Well, I can pick between dying from my father's goons or moving a head injury. I'll take moving a head injury."

She made a pained noise, but he couldn't worry too much about offending her. There had been a truck following them.

"Okay. Okay." He heard her suck in a breath and let it out. "Can you unbuckle yourself?"

He moved and though it was tricky between the pain and dizziness and not being able to see, he managed to unlatch the belt. "Get the gun out of my glove compartment."

He could hear her following instructions, but his vision wasn't magically clearing up. He couldn't focus on that. He couldn't get lost in the now when surviving the next moment was paramount.

How are you going to keep her safe if you can't see?

He'd just have to find a way. "You know how to use it?"

"I can figure it out. Where's the safety?"

He held out his hands and she gingerly placed the gun across his palm. He rubbed his fingers over the gun, pointing out the necessary features.

"It's been years since I've actually done it, and even after Grandma Pauline and Duke taught us, I was never a very good shot."

"Well, unless my sight magically reappears you're all we've got." He handed the gun back to her. "Now, I want you to crawl in the back. I'm going to go out first and—"

"You can't go out first, Cody. You can't *see*."

He opened his mouth to argue. He was the first to jump into a bad situation, the first to risk everything for the safety of others. That was his training and a promise he'd made to himself a long time ago.

But he couldn't see.

"They might be waiting for us to get out. They might grab you, or even hurt you the minute you step out there," Cody replied, but he knew he was only delaying the inevitable. If she wanted to get out of the car, he had no way to stop her.

"I think if they wanted to hurt us they could have done it already if they're out there. I'll carefully creep out and see if I can see anything. You stay put."

Stay put. *Stay put?* He'd never stayed *put* in his entire life. But he didn't have much of a choice since reaching out yielded him nothing but air. He could hear movements, but he couldn't see.

The simple fact lodged like panic in his gut, so he closed his eyes. One step at a time. Always take everything one step at a time.

The first was to get out of the car.

"I don't see anyone," Nina said. "We're in something of a ravine. They had to have seen us go over, but if they're watching from the road, the car is positioned in such a way we should be able to get out without detection. The car is cover. Let's try to get you out. Now you'll have to crawl over the console. Can you—"

"Just tell me if I'm heading the wrong way," he interrupted through gritted teeth. He moved his body and used his hands to feel his way over the console and into the passenger seat. His body throbbed, but the pain there had nothing on the pain in his head, which led him to believe the head injury was the only major injury he'd sustained.

Once he felt the edge of the seat, he got himself into a normal sitting position on it and carefully slung one leg outside, feeling around for the ground. Once he gained purchase, he managed to launch himself onto his feet.

The wave of dizziness threatened to take him down, but Nina's arms came around him.

"I can't call for help. My phone was crushed in the crash. I don't think… I don't think my text to Jamison sent in time," she said, her voice cracking at the end.

"Mine's in my back pocket."

"Don't. I'll get it," she said when he tried to reach for it. "We need to get you cleaned up," she muttered as she slid his phone out of his pocket. "How do you have service? I'm calling 911."

"You can't call 911. Call Jamison."

"You can't see!"

She really needed to stop saying that. He huffed out a breath. "We can't call an ambulance, but I know someone who can help. Go into my contacts." He wavered on his feet feeling unaccountably weak. But then he talked her through finding the hidden contacts on his phone and had her call Shay. She put the phone in his hand and he held it to his nonbloody ear.

"You've got to stop—" Shay answered.

"I've got a serious problem, Shay. I need help."

"I can't help you, Cody. I've done everything I can and—"

"I've been in an accident. I'm pretty sure one or more of Ace's men will have us soon enough. We just need some extrication."

"Extrication. We?" He could hear her mutter something irritable. "Coordinates?"

"Hold on." He turned toward Nina, only knowing where she was because she still had her arm around him helping him stay upright. "Where are we?"

"I don't… I don't know."

"Are you okay?" Shay demanded in his ear.

"Little hurt."

"How little?"

Cody paused.

"That bad, huh?"

He ignored that and explained to her where they'd been driving. About where he thought they went off the highway.

"Hang tight," Shay said, and he could hear her typing away on the computer she was likely hunched over. "I'll see what I can do. We've got a place not far from there. I'll send you a map."

"I can't…see."

"You can't *what*?"

"I'm sure it's temporary, but at the moment I can't see. At all."

"I can read a map," Nina muttered.

"Who is that?" Shay demanded in his ear.

"Nina."

Shay swore. "I'll send the map. Have her follow it. I'll see if I can get anyone out to you."

"A doctor of some kind wouldn't be turned down."

"Ask for the moon why don't you. Get moving. Run into trouble… Hell, I don't know. Just—"

"We'll figure it out. A map and some help and we'll figure it out."

"Turn on your locator."

"Yes, ma'am."

"Things are really bad when you ma'am me. Be careful, Cody." She disconnected and Cody held out the phone. He talked Nina through turning on his locator that he should have deleted after North Star had kicked him out but hadn't.

Thank God for that.

"Cody."

"If you tell me I need an ambulance one more time—"

"Someone's coming," Nina said in low tones. "And they've got a very big gun."

Chapter Twelve

The man picking his way down the ravine took his time, and fear paralyzed Nina for longer than she wanted to admit.

Cody was *blind*, and so bloody and weak she wanted to break down and cry.

But much like that night when someone had broken into her house, she couldn't let fear win. She had to protect the people she loved. She'd killed for Brianna, and she had no doubt she would kill for Cody.

But that didn't make it easy, and it certainly didn't lessen the fear.

"How many?" Cody demanded.

"I only see one. How many were in the truck following us?"

"I only saw one, but there could have been more. You're going to have to shoot him before he gets any closer."

Nina swallowed. She'd always been a terrible shot, but she had to try.

"Use the car as a shield. Don't open yourself up to

getting shot back," Cody was instructing. "You've got a few bullets, so just keep pulling the trigger till you hit."

"And if I don't?"

"We fight."

Nina looked at Cody. He couldn't fight. He was blind, weak, probably from the loss of *all* that blood. She *had* to shoot this person. Which meant she couldn't shake or be frozen like she currently was.

"Talk me through it."

He didn't even hesitate. He nodded. "Find a place where you can see him, but you're hidden as much as possible behind the car."

She did so, and it took too many seconds for her to realize he couldn't *see* that she'd done it. She had to tell him.

"How do you aim?"

"Look for the white circle, then you're trying to get that lined up with the open square. Get it on our guy. Take a deep breath, then pull the trigger. Keep shooting till he stops moving."

Luckily the terrain was uneven at best, which kept the man's progress slow. He was dressed all in black and was much bigger than the man she'd killed in her house back in Dyner.

"Breathe. Breathe and count. Whatever keeps you calm and steady," Cody was explaining in a calm, quiet voice. "You can do it."

She took deep breaths and let them out. She still shook, but as she lined up the sight to the man who got closer with every second, she focused on Cody's quiet, steady words behind her, talking her through it over and over again.

The first shot shook her some, and didn't hit the target. The man didn't even stop his forward movement as he lifted his own gun and pointed it toward the car. She swore.

"It's okay. Just line up and try again. Make sure you've got cover."

She glanced quickly at Cody. "Get lower," she instructed. Because she was their only hope. She knew Ace's men would kill her. They might leave Cody alive since he was Ace's son, but he wouldn't be treated well.

Brianna needed both her parents for once in her life.

The sound of the other man's gun firing pierced the air only a second before the crash of a bullet hitting the car scared a scream out of her.

"Are you okay?" Cody demanded.

"I'm fine. I'm fine," she muttered, lining up her sight. She focused on the fact that she had to save them, for Brianna, and shot again.

This time the man staggered. He didn't fall, but by the way he looked down at his leg she was pretty sure she'd gotten a hit.

"Hit?"

Nina nodded, then remembered Cody couldn't see. "He's still moving, but he's definitely hurt."

"Shoot again."

She did so, once again focusing on Brianna and doing what she had to do. This time when the bullet landed, the man staggered back and fell to his knees.

"You have to kill him, Nina. It's the only way."

She nodded, and though the shakes had taken her over again, she breathed. In and out until she was steady. She aimed for the man's head.

He fell back immediately. Nina could barely hold on to the gun, she was shaking so hard. "Oh God. Oh God." Somehow in the course of a week or so she'd killed two men.

"It's okay. Focus, Nina. We've got to get to safety. Look at my phone." He explained to her where to find the map the person he'd called would have sent and though she struggled to control her limbs, she managed to do what he told her to do.

"I can't read this," she muttered as the map came into view all lines and blinking dots she didn't understand.

"Press the arrow in the corner," Cody instructed.

She did so and nothing happened. "Now what?"

"We move. The red blinking dot will show us where we're going."

"What is all this high-tech stuff?"

"I'll explain once we have some shelter." He made a frustrated noise. "You're going to have to lead me."

She'd killed two men. They were stranded. Brianna was at the ranch. Safe. Thank God. At the ranch.

"Your brothers are going to come looking for us."

"Send them a message. Brianna is their first priority. Text. Quickly. Use code."

"Code?"

"We can't be too careful at this point. Someone might have followed Jamison and Tucker too—which seems likely if only one man came after us. So text Dev. Type this exactly. 827 period B#1 dash 672."

"What does all that mean?" Nina asked as she typed it all in just as he'd said.

"Dev will know. That's what's important. Now…" He trailed off, frowning.

"You're going to have to hold my hand, I guess," Nina said. It was the only way she could think to lead him. "The ground is really uneven here though, so we have to go slow so you don't fall."

He muttered a few curses under his breath. She reached over and took his hand. She swallowed against fear, against the pain at seeing him so hurt. "I have to watch the map, so you have to inch forward slowly feeling the ground before you take a step. I can't carry you if you twist an ankle."

"I won't twist my damn ankle."

Nina studied the land in front of them, then the map. It'd be a miracle if they made it ten feet, let alone the length of this map's route. A miracle if no other men with guns showed up. A miracle if they survived.

But she'd killed two men. Two men who'd tried to kill her simply because of who she'd fallen in love with as a teenager. Simply because of the father of her child.

Who was blind and bloody and weak at the moment.

Which meant she'd find that miracle no matter what.

IT TOOK HOURS. Cody didn't need a clock or sight to know that. It was interminably slow progress, and Nina's constant encouragement was starting to fade and sound hopelessly empty.

But she kept leading him forward, kept muttering over the map.

He fell twice thanks to the rocky terrain. The second time he got up, he almost passed out, but somehow Nina managed to hold him up while he breathed through the wave of pain trying to take him under.

"Oh, there's something ahead," Nina said. "A cabin." Her voice was raspy. They were both dehydrated. He knew he had lost blood too rapidly, but they didn't have time to fix that. They had to get to safety.

But if Nina saw a cabin it had to be the place Shay had mentioned on the phone.

Nina stopped on a dime. "Someone opened the door," she whispered.

"Describe."

"Uh, medium height. It's a woman, I think. Blonde. She's wearing all black. No weapons that I can see."

"Shay."

"Who?"

"The woman I called. She's here to help."

"She's coming this way. Are you sure she's going to help us?"

It took only a few seconds, but soon he heard Shay's voice.

"Lord, you weren't kidding. You need some *help*."

His knees almost gave out when he felt Shay's hand take his free one. Somehow he and Nina had made it. Alive.

So far. There was still a way to go, but this was such a huge step.

"Come on. We'll get you inside and cleaned up

ASAP," Shay said, her voice no-nonsense and sure, which was a great relief.

"She needs to get checked out too," Cody managed to say despite how raw his throat felt.

"I'm fine," Nina insisted as they kept moving. God he wanted to lie down.

"We'll get you both looked at," Shay returned reassuringly. "Jennings wouldn't approve any of the medical team to come with me, so I had to go for the next best thing."

"Holy hell, brother, what did you do to yourself?"

"Brady?" Cody nearly collapsed at the sound of his brother's voice, but strong arms were holding him up. Not Nina's slim ones or even Shay's capable ones, but his brother's.

"Brianna—"

Brady quickly cut Nina off. "Everyone's at the ranch and accounted for except you two. Tucker and Jamison had tails, but no tampering on their car. Probably because they'd parked next to Gage at the prison. They lost the tails and got home. Everyone, including the Knights, are staying at the ranch until further notice, and Brianna is absolutely under someone's watch 24-7."

While Brady explained that to Nina, he helped Cody sit down. Cody could feel his brother's hands on his face and Cody tried not to wince or give away how badly everything hurt.

"I'm not sure I've got the skills for this," Brady said in practically a whisper. Cody assumed he was trying to keep Nina from hearing.

"Let's get him cleaned up." Shay's voice. "I can

maybe call Betty and see if she can video chat us through making sure he's repairable."

"Of course he's repairable," Nina snapped.

Someone took his hand, and it only took a second or two to realize it was Nina. She murmured encouraging words to him as Brady and Shay spoke in low tones about the extent of his injuries. The pain while they cleaned up his face was nearly unbearable, so he focused on Nina's hand in his and the fact everyone else he loved was keeping Brianna safe.

"I can stitch you up," Brady finally said. "But we don't have any local anesthesia. The real concern is the loss of sight. That could be caused by bleeding in the brain."

Nina's sharp intake of breath next to him had him squeezing her hand. "But it's not the only cause."

"No. It could be permanent or temporary damage to the part of your brain that controls sight."

"Which means my sight could return as it heals."

"*Could*, Cody. Not will. This could be serious."

"*Could be* but not *is*."

Brady muttered curses under his breath.

"How would we get him to a hospital?" Nina asked gently. "I think it's paramount Ace doesn't know he's been hurt, especially this severely."

"We don't *know* it's severe," Cody interrupted.

"We know it's possible though," Brady returned.

"Let me call Betty. She's our resident doc. We can do a secure video chat and she can lead Brady through a more thorough examination. Then we'll decide what kind of interventions we need."

"I don't need any—"

"And you'll shut the hell up, Cody," Shay snapped.

He grunted irritably while Brady and Shay murmured in low tones, before he heard a faraway voice. Presumably Betty on the video call.

"Well, someone did a number on you. And you thought being part of North Star was dangerous, huh?"

"I'm Ace Wyatt's son, Bet. Life is dangerous."

She snorted derisively. Everyone involved with North Star liked to give him crap that he was Ace Wyatt's son, and Cody had become something like immune to the barbs. He was who he was.

He found he wasn't so sanguine about what and who he was with Nina holding his hand.

Shay and Brady poked and prodded his face while Betty asked them questions.

"Cody, no sight whatsoever?"

"I can make out some shadows. Sort of."

Betty made a considering noise. She'd patched Jamison up after their last run-in with Dad, and Brady was a skilled EMT, who most definitely could have become a doctor if he'd had the opportunities normal kids did. There was no reason to believe they couldn't patch him up.

He had to be okay. He might not have cared so deeply about surviving a few weeks ago, but he had a daughter now.

"Any other situation, I'd already have you in a hospital. But we're all versed in how dangerous Ace can be, and apparently jail hasn't put an end to his reach. Not that any of us thought it would be that easy."

No, Cody hadn't thought it would be, but he'd hoped. "Brady—what kind of supplies you got?"

Brady and Betty discussed logistics, and eventually ended the call. Even though Cody couldn't see, he could practically feel everyone looking at him, determining his fate.

He really didn't appreciate that feeling. If that didn't make him antsy enough, he heard a door open and close. Footsteps. Low voices. And he had no clue what was going on around him.

He always relied on all of his senses, on being in control of a situation. If he was in charge, no one could get the better of him—most especially Ace.

"Breathe," Nina whispered, and it was only then he realized panic was winning, and no matter what the situation he could not let that happen.

The door opening and closing sounded again, then clanking and thumping noises. "First things first," Brady offered. "Sedatives."

"No."

"I've got to give you stitches—in your face. I'm going to knock you out and you're not going to argue with me over it. Now, Shay and Nina let's move him to a bed. But I'll need good light and help from both of you while I do this."

Cody was led to a bed. Brady belted out instructions, and after the sedative was administered, Cody felt himself unwillingly start to fade. He finally let go into the dark when Nina touched his forehead gently and urged him to go to sleep.

When he woke later it was to searing pain on top of

deep, throbbing pain and a very dry mouth. He moved and for a second thought he was in a dark room before he remembered—oh right, he couldn't see.

He was in bed and there was something warm and soft next to him. It moved.

"I really hope this is Nina and not my brother," he said, wincing at the pain in his throat and how ragged he felt.

"What about Shay?"

Cody shifted uncomfortably. "I said Nina, didn't I?"

Nina made a considering noise, but she didn't move away from him. She snuggled closer. "How are you feeling?"

"Dandy."

Her laugh was soft, muted, but it made him feel marginally better. "How long have I been out?"

"A couple hours. It's about midnight. You should try to sleep more if you can."

"Did they ever look you over?"

"Yes. Brady rebandaged my stitches, and a few other scrapes I got from the accident, but he said I was fine."

"You're not lying to a blind man, are you?"

"Not right now."

He relaxed some. She was okay and that was what was important.

"Sleep," she ordered.

"Have you been sleeping?"

Nina sighed. "I'm trying."

"You're worried." He could hear it in her voice—the tightness, the exhaustion. She was trying to hold it all together for him, because he was hurt. But hurt or no, blind or no, he would do everything to keep Nina from suffering.

"Do you think she's scared?" Nina asked after a long, interminable silence.

She didn't have to say *Brianna* for him to know who she was talking about. "She has everyone but us rallied around her. I'm sure she's worried about you, but she's safe. That's the important thing right now." He tried to believe that instead of thinking of all the ways she was only unsafe because of him.

"She loves you, Cody."

It was dark—or he couldn't see—but it felt like the very same thing, and Nina was curled up beside him like they hadn't lost seven years. Like those years didn't exist. Part of him didn't want them to.

But they did.

He wanted to believe there was some magic connection between father and child—so that he could believe Brianna had just loved him on sight, but that only meant there was something connecting him to Ace.

He didn't love his father. Maybe his feelings had been complicated as a child, but he'd never *loved* Ace.

"If she loves me, it's only because of you."

"I tried to give her everything I would have wanted her to have. I wanted her to have you, but I didn't think she could. So I did the best I could, but they were just stories."

"Stories that gave her a foundation of trust. We both know how hard trust is when you grow up in a dangerous situation, and you gave that to her."

Her breathing hitched, but when she spoke, her voice

was steady even if there was fear behind her words. "Cody, what if—"

"No what-ifs. One step at a time. We're going to get through this. It'll be hard, and yeah we might get hurt in the process, but we're going to get through to the other side safer and better off."

She was quiet for a moment, but he could feel her fingers curl around his hand. "And together," she whispered.

"Yeah." Together. A family. He wasn't sure quite what to do with that yet, so he slid back into sleep instead.

Chapter Thirteen

When Nina woke up she was achy. Not just from the stitched-up wound in her stomach, but all over. Her neck throbbed along with a pain at the base of her skull. When she slid out of bed, she nearly collapsed at the pain in her knees and feet.

She managed to steady herself and glanced at Cody in the dim light of the room. It had to be morning, but he needed his sleep. The white bandages had spots of blood bleeding through, and his complexion was so waxen.

Brady had assured her he'd come through, but it was hard to believe looking at him like this.

So she couldn't. She slid out of the room and headed for the kitchen. She'd get some coffee hopefully, try to remind herself of all she'd fought for and would continue to, and when she returned to Cody's side she'd be ready to have a determined outlook.

Nina stopped abruptly at the sight of the woman in the kitchen. She didn't know what to make of Shay or the way Cody talked to her.

Or how the similarities between them made even

her uncomfortable. Same color blond hair, same color blue eyes. Shay was taller, but they had the same kind of build.

"Morning," Shay offered. "Coffee's on. Help yourself."

"Thank you."

"And ibuprofen," Shay added with a small smile, pushing a bottle toward the coffeepot.

"Bless you." Nina fought off discomfort and moved into the kitchen. Shay shoved something into a big duffel bag and then hefted the strap onto her shoulder.

"You're leaving?" Nina asked, surprised and maybe a little afraid they were losing this woman who seemed so sure of everything.

"I have to get back. North Star controls my life, and this was a blip they're not going to easily forgive. I've got some major groveling to do."

"But you helped us. You saved us."

Shay's lips twisted wryly. "It wasn't part of the mission I was supposed to be involved with."

"Then why did you help us?"

The woman shrugged. "Cody's a good guy."

Something uncomfortable turned in Nina's stomach, but she didn't have a right to that, so she tried to push it away. "I…"

"I'm going to go out on a limb and guess he's been pretty tight-lipped about everything, but nothing ever happened between us."

"Oh. Right. I didn't…" It was none of her business. She hadn't been with Cody. She had absolutely no hold on him those seven years she'd been hiding. Jealousy was dumb, feeling relieved by Shay's words was worse. Shay seeming to read her thoughts was embarrassing. Still, it didn't seem to shut her up. "Why not?"

"We would have gotten kicked out of the group." Shay raised her shoulder as if that was that. "Neither of us could afford to lose North Star."

"Then you didn't want each other very much." At the look Shay gave her, Nina turned a deep shade of red. "It's none of my business. I'm sorry."

"No, you're right. I suppose we didn't. Never really thought of it that way. Anyway, I've got to go or I'm canned for nothing."

"It wasn't for nothing. Thank you."

Shay nodded, slinging a bag over her shoulder. "Ace is a dangerous man. Don't underestimate him."

"I don't."

"Sometimes they do," she replied, nodding toward the back of the cabin where Cody was asleep and presumably so was Brady. "A guy thing or a being-his-son thing. I don't know. But Ace underestimates them too, so I guess they're even. Unfortunately when men get even, women often get the shaft. No matter how good some of the men involved are. Watch out for yourself, Nina."

Nina nodded, even as the words settled uncomfortably on her shoulders—a scary, truthful weight.

Shay left the cabin and Nina was left alone in the kitchen. She got her coffee, took the painkillers and listened carefully for Cody waking up while her thoughts of Ace, Shay and Cody being blind whirled in her head.

"How's our patient?"

She looked up at Brady and tried to smile. "Still sleeping." She sipped her coffee. "Will you be honest with me and tell me how bad it really is?"

He pressed his lips together. His eyes were sad, but he held her gaze. "I don't know how bad it is. Truthfully. I wish we could get him to a hospital, and maybe we'll be able to soon enough. But we have to make sure Ace doesn't know. Ace can't know."

That had been a tenet in her life for so long, and it turned out it didn't matter. Ace *had* known about Brianna.

Nina swallowed against the way that realization just kept *hurting* like a brand-new wave of pain. She looked at her coffee. "As long as Ace's alive, Brianna isn't safe. None of us are."

"You know, you could take Duke's suggestion. Move to some remote area. Disappear. Ace has reach, but not that kind of reach."

"He'll find a way. Maybe not for ten years, but he'd find a way. The only answer is Ace's death."

"We can't make that happen while he's in jail."

"Unless he gets the death penalty." Nina looked up at Brady, a desperate hope clawing through her. "He could, couldn't he?"

"What he's in jail for right now involves trafficking. No death penalty there."

"But he's killed people. We know that."

"We know that, but we can't prove that. Gage and I have talked about this some. We'd need a lot more evidence to make a bigger charge stick. Ace is careful, and he has a lot of men doing the work for him. It's nearly impossible."

"Unless we get one of those men."

"And do what? Torture some answers out of him?"

Nina lifted a shoulder. "To save my daughter? Yeah. I've killed two men, and it may have been self-defense, Brady, but I'd kill a hundred more to keep her safe."

She could tell she'd surprised him, but motherhood had changed her. Ace had changed her. She'd do whatever it took, with no moral qualms, to keep her child safe.

"One hundred won't be necessary."

At Cody's voice she and Brady immediately jumped into action, moving to help him to the table—though somehow he'd made it out of bed and the bedroom.

"You can see?" Nina demanded, her heart beating so hard with hope.

"No. I can feel the walls and move toward voices," Cody replied wryly. "Even over the lovely pounding in my head. I smell coffee."

"I'll get it," Brady offered.

Nina led Cody to the table, helping him get settled on a chair and Brady put a mug in front of him. Nina gently placed his hand around the handle.

"I'm not used to being waited on," Cody finally said when no one spoke.

"I wouldn't plan on getting used to it," Brady replied.

Nina frowned at Brady, but he only shrugged, and Cody's mouth curved upward. She supposed the warped way the brothers were hard on each other was some comfort to Cody right now.

"Shay left?"

Nina nodded, then remembered Cody couldn't see. "Yeah, just a bit ago."

"Good."

"Is it?" Brady asked.

Cody shrugged. "For her. For North Star. I can't keep leaning on them for help."

"I don't understand why not. If they're trying to bring Ace down, I don't understand why you just get kicked out and left in the cold."

"Because they're trying to bring the Sons down, not Ace in particular. I had a use and now it's done. Look, this is our fight. Ace is our fight."

"You're blind, Cody. And stuck in this cabin... Who even owns this place?"

"It's fine," Cody replied.

Nina could tell Brady wanted to argue, but he clamped his mouth shut and scowled instead.

"It occurred to me while listening to you guys talk, we're so focused on Ace, we're missing an important part of this puzzle." Carefully he lifted the mug of coffee to his mouth and sipped, Nina and Brady leaning more and more forward as they waited for him to finish that thought.

"The men he's getting to do his dirty work?" Brady supplied impatiently.

Cody slowly lowered the mug and shook his head. "Not his goons. They don't have access to him, but someone does who's passing along information."

"It could be a guard, I guess?" Brady suggested.

"Or one of his lawyers."

"Weren't they court appointed?"

"One was, and North Star couldn't find any information passing, but Jamison said he had lawyers coming to visit him—plural. He was looking into them, but we got sidetracked with the whole go see Ace thing. We need to look into these lawyers. And the great thing about lawyers is they know just how to twist the law."

"Okay. But what do *we* do? Right here?"

Cody lifted the mug again. "We give them what they want."

THIS IS HIS head injury talking, isn't it?" Nina demanded, her voice leaning toward shrill. "He didn't just say that."

It was strange to have to live in this world of only gray. To depend on his hearing and his touch to understand what was going on around him. But something about that kept him calm. Kept him centered—not in fear, but in the reality of the situation. He couldn't see the hurt in her blue eyes, so he could breathe. He could think. "Nina. Hear me out."

"How can you be so calm?" she demanded. "You're sitting there blind and hurt. I've been shot. My daughter is—"

"Safe," Cody and Brady interrupted in tandem.

"They hurt both of us. Why should I believe she's safe?"

Her voice broke at that. He couldn't reach out and

touch her. He'd come up with nothing but air, because even though he knew she sat to his right he couldn't *see*.

"There is nowhere she'd be safer than at the ranch, with both our families watching out for her. I think you know that. There's no place we could hide her that he couldn't reach. So we have to protect her. And we all would do anything to keep her safe."

"It isn't enough," Nina said, though her voice had roughened into a whisper.

"We're all still alive. Still here. We have scars—all of us—Jamison, Dev, you and me. But we've survived. Because we believed we could and fought to. We just have to keep fighting."

"By giving them what they want?"

"Ace wants us hurt. Weak. Rattled. He wants us afraid, and he wants us to make a mistake. So he can punish me. It's all part of it. He likes the game as much as the punishment—it's why he can wait so long to enact it."

"So, you let him believe you're hurt, weak and rattled?" Brady replied. "I hate to break it to you, brother…"

"I know. We are those things, but we'd usually try to hide it. What if we didn't. What if, instead of hiding everything beneath pride and some desperate need to show him up, we let him believe he's getting what he wants?"

"He *is*," Nina replied, but her voice didn't break. She sounded more contemplative than angry or terrified.

"It doesn't matter. Not in the long run. The mistake I made in that jail? It was getting mad. It was reacting.

It was trying to show him up. He made that comment about Brianna to trick me into admitting I knew about her, and he won because I wanted to prove to him he would never touch her."

"Okay," Brady said, and Cody knew he was trying to sound thoughtful instead of dismissive.

"Let's go with this thread. How do we use Ace knowing you're hurt to our advantage?"

"We need to catch him in the act. Which means, we need to have him thinking it's the time to strike, and we see how he's getting messages out of the jail."

"This second lawyer."

"Exactly. I'll want Jamison, Dev and Gage at the ranch with Brianna and the girls. We want the most presence there. But Tucker can look into this lawyer, while you find a way to get someone from the Sons to suspect you're helping patch me up."

Cody wished he could see his brother's face. Brady was good at keeping his feelings close to the vest, but Cody would know his response to the plan.

"It won't work."

Cody frowned in Nina's direction. "It could."

"Not if you have three of your brothers stationed at the ranch. Ace won't make a move for Brianna when she's that protected. He'll wait. He'll wait it out."

"She has a point," Brady offered. "He doesn't want you dead. He wants you hurt. He wants to punish you. Dev's still alive for a reason. He'd leave you alive for the same."

Cody wanted to shove away from the table. He

wanted to pace. He wanted to *act*. But he couldn't in his condition.

He could just hear the words his brother wasn't saying rattle around in his head.

He'd leave you alive for the same...but he'd kill Brianna and Nina to hurt you.

No. He wouldn't allow it. "If he thinks we're weak, he'll make a mistake." Cody believed that wholeheartedly. Ace *had* made a mistake yesterday, or at least a slipup. He'd admitted the first man Nina had killed had blundered the kidnapping. Ace would have never wanted them to know he failed—even if he did blame it on an underling.

But how long could they wait around for Ace to make a move? Ace had the gift of time. Cody didn't—because he had a little girl who deserved a real life.

He heard Nina take a sharp inhale, then slowly let it out. He wanted to place his hand over hers. Offer some kind of comfort, but he didn't know where to reach and he couldn't bring himself to fumble.

"He's not going to act just because we're weak," Nina said quietly. "Surely we've been weak before. He wants a specific thing. He wants to use Brianna to hurt you."

He'd worked very hard not to blame himself for his father's vices, for his father's evil. Sometimes he was so afraid he had that evil in him, but he chose to turn away from it. Which meant he wouldn't lay blame on himself for Ace's choices.

But Brianna being in the crosshairs of this hell *was*

his fault. There was no getting around that. Being his daughter meant she'd always be Ace's target.

"I don't say that to hurt you," Nina said quietly.

"It's the truth. Regardless of hurt," he replied, trying to keep his emotions out of it. Harder when he had nothing to look at but gray, when he remembered what it had felt like to read Brianna a story while she curled up next to him.

He heard Nina sigh, and could almost feel her wanting to argue with him. But maybe that was all wishful thinking. It wasn't as if he could examine her expression and see what was going on there.

"Fine. Regardless of hurt. We let Ace know we're weak. We give him the leeway to make a mistake, but he has to be motivated to use that leeway now. Which means he has to think Brianna is weak too. Obviously, we can't ever let her be, but maybe we can make him *think* she is. What if he thinks we have Brianna? Here. Unguarded. Just the two of us, hurt and on the run. What would he do if he thought we were trying to run with her?"

Chapter Fourteen

Just the idea made Nina sick to her stomach, but if yesterday had taught her anything, it was that this had to end.

End.

"He'd send someone after you," Brady said. "But... It'd require a lot of subterfuge to make it actually look like you guys had Brianna. It would take... I'm not sure it's possible."

"It doesn't have to be possible," Cody replied, nodding along with what Nina had said. "What does trying lose us?"

"I want to point out you're both hurt. Severely. Nina's gunshot wound might be last week's news, but that's still a serious injury. There's a lot to lose."

"As long as Brianna is safe, we haven't lost anything," Nina replied.

"But what will she lose?"

What would Brianna lose? Nina tried not to think that far. If she started counting all the things Brianna had already lost, she'd be crushed under the weight of it.

"Nothing," Cody said, his voice harsh even as his unseeing eyes stared straight ahead. "I won't allow Brianna to lose a damn thing."

It wasn't that the violence in his tone surprised her. She knew Cody had all sorts of violence in him. She knew, simply from watching them together, that he loved Brianna with no reservations. She knew he would protect her, because his own honor demanded it. But she was starting to realize that no matter the years she'd kept Brianna's existence from him, he would protect her not just because he had to, but because he loved his daughter unreservedly.

If she let herself linger in that wonder, she'd have to look too hard at her own parents' failures and be buried under the weight of *that*. So she studied his face—bruised and bandaged.

That bandage needed to be changed. He needed a real doctor and probably some kind of scan to look at the damage to his brain likely causing the loss of sight. He needed this to be over.

They all did.

"So, how can we make that happen? How can we make Ace think we have her, and that we're running away?" Nina asked, turning her gaze to Brady.

They spent the next hour or so coming up with ideas, rejecting most of them. Brady went about changing Cody's bandages and examining his eyes as they plotted.

But no matter how many plans they came up with, they kept running into the same problem.

"How is Ace going to know we're doing this? We

keep working under the assumption he's watching our every move. I don't think that's true. Clearly there are limits to what he can accomplish—at least with time constraints," Brady said.

"We have to find out more about this attorney," Cody replied to his brother. "Use that angle. We need to go at this from multiple fronts."

Nina watched them. Both men seemed to pulse with excess energy—Cody unable to pace like she was almost sure he would be doing if he could see. Brady keeping still whether out of deference to Cody or because it was simply his personality.

"The more fronts we go after, the more we leave Brianna unprotected. We can't all be on the ranch if we're pulling on these threads."

Cody rubbed a hand over the side of his face that wasn't bandaged.

"So, we have the attorney thread," Nina said, holding up one finger. "Jamison is the one most likely to tackle that."

"Making it look like someone got Brianna to you guys, or you got Brianna from the ranch—all while making it look like we're trying to be sneaky," Brady said, adding another finger to the list. "You'd need more than one of us. Likely me and Gage."

"Tuck should also look into these men who've come after us. Maybe he can get someone to talk. Bodies are piling up. You really want to be next while Ace cools his heels in a cell?"

Nina held up a finger for him since he didn't know they were silently counting.

"That only leaves Dev at the ranch to protect Brianna." Brady shook his head. "We can't go after all those threads at once and leave her that open."

"That's insulting."

Brady raised his eyebrows at her. "How so?"

"You're underestimating everyone who doesn't have a magical genital gift between their legs."

Brady tilted his head toward Cody even though Cody couldn't see. "Did she really just say *magical genital gift?*" Brady asked, his voice tinged with both horror and amusement.

Nina didn't have time for either. "Grandma Pauline is probably just as good a shot as any of you boys, if not better. Liza held her own in the Sons for years. Cecilia is a police officer, for God's sake. You're ignoring the fact we have very capable women able and willing to keep my daughter safe."

"Our daughter. *Our* daughter safe," Cody returned, his voice so cold she almost shivered. "Excuse me if I trust my brothers first and foremost."

Though she felt the sting of that rebuff, and guilt that she *had* used *my* instead of *our*, she kept her response to the point. "Excuse *me* if I trust my sisters just as much."

"She's right," Brady said, though his voice was quiet, almost as if he was trying to talk to Cody without her hearing. "Liza and Cec and Dev, plus Grandma and Duke? She'll be protected."

Cody was quiet, and whatever he was thinking or feeling, Nina couldn't read. So she didn't try. She let silence settle around them, everyone waiting for Cody to talk.

"You'll have to go," he finally offered in Brady's direction.

"Excuse me? I'm not leaving you guys."

"Gage can't cause a diversion *and* make it look like he got Brianna out all on his own. He needs help," Cody returned.

"Rachel, Sarah and Felicity."

"A half-blind woman, a timid park ranger and Sarah—who'd chop off Ace's nose to spite all our faces?"

Cody's mouth curved. "Say that to their face?"

"Not a chance in hell," Brady muttered, shoving away from the table. Irritation simmered off him in waves, and Nina had to resist the urge to return with exasperation in kind.

Rachel, Sarah and Felicity could take anyone Brady threw at them. Unfortunately, they weren't the answer here.

"Let's think like Ace for a second," Nina replied, ignoring the disgusted snorts from both men she was stuck in this little cabin with. "We know he doesn't think much of women. I think he might be afraid of Grandma Pauline, but mostly he sees the rest of us as pawns. Pawns to get to you boys. It'll be you boys he's watching, and it'll be you boys he expects to do the work. If we really wanted to get Brianna out of there, we'd go with people he wouldn't expect. But we're trying to play into his hands."

Brady heaved out a sigh. "Play into his hands without him seeing through it."

"Yes," Nina agreed. "But we've talked about Ace's weakness being his pride. His focus, his obsession, is his children. He wanted me dead." This time, she couldn't quite suppress a shudder. "He made that clear back there in that prison. I should be dead. Because I don't matter to him." She forced herself to say the next part. "But Brianna does."

"*Matter* isn't the word I'd use, Nina."

"Well, I don't want to argue semantics, Cody. I want this over. We all do. So, Brady. You'll go. You'll lay out the plan for everyone. Once Jamison has a few leads on the lawyer, and can be sure he'll be watching or having someone watch so he can feed messages to Ace, you and Gage enact a plan to make it look like you're bringing Brianna here."

"And if some of his goons find you first?" Brady returned.

"We can protect ourselves, injuries or not," Cody replied. "We've gotten this far. Besides, this is a North Star property. There are weapons and security measures here."

Nina frowned. "Shay made it sound like she might get kicked out for helping. But they'll let you stay here?"

Cody shrugged negligently.

"That is *not* an answer, Cody Wyatt."

Brady snorted. "That is *some* mom voice."

Nina glared at him and he held up his hands in surrender.

"I can't get into it. It's North Star business, but we've got this place for a few days. While we're here, we can use their security systems and their weapons."

"You'll want it to look like you're getting ready to move. To run. You'll need a vehicle," Brady mused.

"I'm guessing it won't be my truck."

"Make it part of the fake getting Brianna to us," Nina suggested. "Come in two cars. Leave one."

Brady nodded. "What about communication?"

"We've got to be careful. No texts. Phone calls should be all right, as long as they're in safe locations. I don't think Ace has the power right now to do much more than follow and threaten. Tech's going to be beyond his reach, but we should still be careful."

"I think you're right, and we'll all be careful. I guess we should start."

Cody nodded. "Thanks for the patch up."

Brady scowled, studying Cody's damaged face. "You need a real doctor."

"You do in a pinch."

Brady shook his head in disgust. "Let's end this quick so someone can check out that head wound, huh?"

"I'm all for quick as long as Brianna's safe."

Brady grunted, nodded toward Nina. "I'll get my stuff together and head out." He walked back into the hallway and to the room he must have stayed in.

Nina knew Cody couldn't see, but his gaze was on his clasped hands in front of him. Some of his stoic surety had faded—likely in knowing Brady would be gone and she'd be his best hope for survival. Probably not a pleasant thought.

But she'd protect him, just as she'd protected Brianna.

Love swept through her, a painful reminder that for these past seven years she had existed in a kind of cage. She'd kept moving forward, kept protecting her daughter, but on the inside she was the same woman who'd loved this man.

She opened her mouth to tell him she'd keep him safe, but then thought better of it. That would be no comfort to him. She didn't know what would be—so she did the only thing she could think of.

She got out of her chair and leaned close to his face. She'd only meant to kiss his cheek. A kind of reassurance, a sign this was as okay as it could be. But he angled his head, as if he heard her next to him. She could have stopped herself, if she'd wanted to.

But she didn't want to.

So she brushed her lips against his instead.

Lips brushed his and Cody's heart seemed to shudder to a stop, like a car slipping a gear. He thought maybe he could have handled it somehow if he could see, but blind there was only sensation and that was very, very dangerous.

So he held himself still. As much as he wanted to reach out, how could he? He didn't know exactly where she was. When he could think, puzzle out what they would do, he didn't panic despite the loss of eyesight.

But in *this*, a sensation he'd missed for seven years

no matter how often he'd told himself he didn't want or need it, seeing nothing was only panic.

He could hear what were presumably his brother's footsteps even over the beating of his rioting heart.

Nina didn't move, and all Cody could seem to do was wonder how she looked. He wasn't even sure if she was standing or sitting—he only knew she was close enough to touch—and he didn't know how to reach her.

"For the record, no one is going to like this plan," Brady said. "I'll be lucky if I even explain it to them before the arguing takes over."

"Get lucky then." Cody tried to aim a smile in Brady's direction. "Watch your back, brother."

"Let Nina watch yours," Brady replied.

Cody didn't say anything to that, didn't say anything at all until he heard a door swing open and then click shut.

He heard Nina's expelled whoosh of breath—a kind of release of tension even as a new one settled around them.

They were alone. Their hands were tied until someone else acted.

She had kissed him.

He was blind.

Brady's words *let Nina watch yours*.

It scraped him raw. It wasn't that he didn't trust her, didn't believe her capable. She'd kept Brianna safe from Ace—whether for seven whole years or just stabbing a man after she'd been shot—it was quite the feat.

But he wanted to be the one saving. He hadn't saved

her seven years ago. If anything, by disappearing and never telling him about Brianna, she'd saved him then.

What had he ever done for her except bring her here? Away from their daughter. Injured. With a man who couldn't fully protect her.

The scrape of chair against floor interrupted the quiet, the table wiggling underneath his arms.

"I don't understand this North Star group," Nina blurted out, clearly agitated. "How can they threaten to fire Shay when she's helping you? How can they not help you when they want to bring Ace down?"

"They don't want to bring Ace down," Cody replied calmly. It was easy to be calm when talking about facts. And ignoring that a kiss so sweet and feather-light made him feel like he'd been asleep all those seven years he thought he'd been doing the most important work of his life.

"I thought you said…"

"They want to end the Sons," Cody explained, as he'd had to explain to all of his brothers at one point or another the past two months. "It's their mission to demolish the group. So, yeah, taking Ace down is part of it sometimes. But while he's in jail, their focus is the Sons—not Ace, and certainly not his actual children. Personal vendettas aren't their problem."

"Personal vendettas? Is that what you'd call it?"

"No, I'd call it a psychotic episode. It certainly isn't simple sociopathy. Regardless. It *is* personal. It's not about the Sons. That group and their drugs and weapons, and trafficking of all that, *and* their attempts to get into human trafficking are the real target of the North

Star group. By abandoning my mission and helping Jamison and Liza *over* the North Star mission, I got myself kicked out."

"Did they expect you to turn your back on your brother?" Nina demanded incredulously.

"No. They didn't. But expecting me to turn my back on my brother and being able to use me for their missions are two different things. I'm too personally connected now. They can't trust me to do what *they're* trying to do. Which doesn't just jeopardize their mission, but the lives of everyone on any one of my teams."

"It isn't fair," Nina replied, and it eased some of the tension in him that she sounded somewhat petulant. "It isn't right."

"It is to them, and for them," he replied, his tone gentler than he'd intended.

He heard a sound—maybe her plopping back onto the chair—and a harrumph. "I hate when you're all detached and reasonable," she muttered. "I don't know how to do that."

"Because you haven't been trying to take down anyone. You've been trying to keep our daughter safe."

"She's safe," Nina said quietly, but there was a tremor to her voice. As if she was saying it to reassure herself. To seek his reassurance.

Which was the only reason he pushed out his arm, held his palm up. He didn't know how to reach for her hand, or her. He didn't have words. So he had to reach out and trust she would too.

Her hand slid into his. He squeezed it. "She's safe. Our families will keep her safe."

He wished he could see her. Judge if that gave her any reassurance. Was she pale and exhausted like she'd been back at the ranch? She hadn't been knocked out like he'd been…maybe she hadn't slept.

He opened his mouth to tell her to do just that, but she spoke first.

"How come nothing ever happened between you and Shay?"

Embarrassingly, he jolted. It was a pointless question, with an easy answer, and yet the way Nina asked it into this gray mist that was all that existed around him right now… It knocked him back.

Nina's hand closed tighter around his, as if she was afraid he'd walk away.

If he'd been able to see, he would have. But of course he couldn't. So he had to sit there.

"It would have risked our jobs."

"That's what she said. She brought it up. The whole you two not ever… Well."

Cody *really* didn't know what to say to that.

"I don't buy it."

"Excuse me?"

"On her end, maybe. But if there'd really been something there—something enough for Shay to mention it, and you to act tense about it when I do—there has to be something more than your jobs."

"North Star wasn't just a job. Not to me." Which was true. Beside the point, but true.

"Maybe not." She was quiet for so many seconds he thought he'd be able to pull his hands away and escape. He thought wrong.

"I know you, Cody. Maybe you've changed. I haven't. I've been stuck in the same place, where everything I am is survival. The only parts of me that have changed are the lengths I'm willing to go to protect the people I love. But that's not change. Not real change. I still know the boy you would've been when you joined North Star and it doesn't add up."

"You've always been bad at math," he replied.

"I want a real answer."

"Why? What does any of this matter?" He tried to ignore the simmering irritation, but this line of conversation, plus the throbbing pain in his body, and the situation that required him to sit here and *wait* made that very difficult. "What would it matter if Shay and I had a relationship? This has nothing to do with the task at hand."

"The task at hand is to sit here and wait to see how we can make your father think we have our daughter," Nina replied. "We can't do anything until wheels are set in motion."

"So…you want to what? Take a tour of our romantic detours the past seven years?"

"No," she replied, the reasonableness in her tone setting his teeth on edge. "I'm asking you a specific question about a specific woman."

"What do you want me to say?" Cody demanded, his frustration with *everything* bubbling over at this *one* thing she kept poking at. "That she looked like you? That sometimes out of the corner of my eye it'd be like a ghost was there. That I was never certain if that attraction I felt was her, or still wanting you? Is that what you want to hear?"

She was wholly silent. He didn't even hear her breathe until she spoke. "I only wanted the truth," she said quietly, a pinched quality to each word as if she was in pain.

As if *she* was in pain.

"Well the damn truth is it was still wanting you. It always will be. You're the only one I've ever wanted."

Chapter Fifteen

Every word Cody spoke seemed to strike her with such force that her breath got caught in her lungs. She couldn't move for a good minute or so as she absorbed the words. Then it took another minute for her body to stop reacting to each blow.

She didn't know why she'd suddenly felt she had to understand the whole *Shay* thing. The woman had said nothing had happened. That whatever attraction there'd been had been incidental, unimportant. So, why should Nina care what Cody had rightfully done in the seven years they'd been apart?

She didn't care.

Okay, she didn't *want* to care. And it turned out Nina didn't care what Shay felt or thought or said about nothing happening or why. She only cared what Cody felt. Not then. Here and now. Was there any of *this* left over inside of him too? Could that be what had really held him back when it had come to Shay?

She'd wanted it to be true, but knew it couldn't possibly be. She'd had to hear him say it to get rid of all that awful hope.

Maybe she'd secretly believed he'd say something about her being hard to get over or something vague but comforting.

She hadn't expected anger.

She really hadn't expected being the *only* one.

He'd said *you're* like it was present tense. Like in this moment, she was his only one. It washed over her and through her, all that terrifying hope she'd been trying to avoid.

Wasn't everything she hoped for always too good to be true?

Not Brianna.

Six years with that beautiful girl. They'd been terrifying years—always afraid the next move would mean she'd lose her. Because Brianna was too good to be true, and yet for six years she'd been true—and now Nina had so many people working to make sure it would be true. Period.

Brianna was still here. Still hers—and now theirs. Brianna finally got to have Cody, and Nina wanted to have him too, no matter how unfair it might be.

You're the only one I've ever wanted.

"You're going to have to let a blind man know if you walk out of the room, Nina."

"I didn't walk out," she managed to reply despite how tight her throat felt. "I'm trying to…" Her breath shuddered out, betraying all the emotion battling it out inside of her. "I don't…"

"You don't," he said flatly.

"No! No. I… Cody." She raked her hands through her hair trying to get a handle on the here and now and not her circling thoughts. She could cry if she wanted to. He wouldn't see it. She could indeed slip out of the room and never have this conversation. She had all the power here.

But hadn't she already lost seven years? Why wouldn't she use her power to do something about *that*?

"You're telling me after I left you the way I did," she said, wincing at how her voice shook, and how much the memory still hurt. "After I *lied* to you the way I did, I'm still the only person you've ever wanted? We lost all that time. I kept Brianna from you."

"Yes. You concealed her. We lost. Seven years passed." He said that all in his detached way, but emotion was creeping into his expression, into each word. "Too much has changed and passed, and I can tell myself that from here to eternity. It doesn't seem to change how I feel."

"I never stopped," Nina whispered, despite the fact that tears burned her eyes, that her throat felt as if someone was squeezing the breath out of her.

All he'd mentioned was want, not love.

"Stopped what?" he muttered, clearly irritated with the conversation, with himself, with being unable to leave.

But he actually couldn't leave. Not easily in this unfamiliar cabin with a brand-new loss of sight. Which meant she got to say whatever she wanted. After seven years of not being able to tell him *anything*.

"I never stopped loving you."

It was his turn not to speak, even as she waited, desperately wishing he'd say something. Anything. But his unseeing gaze was straight ahead and his expression gave nothing away.

There was just the oppressive silence in this weird little cabin that wasn't theirs. This life that hadn't felt like her own in seven years. How was it she was sitting next to him—both of them injured—having this conversation? Brianna secreted away on the ranch with Duke and Liza and all the girls and Wyatt boys and...

Now wasn't the time, or the place. Brianna should be their focus. They should hatch a million plans until they were all safe and home.

Home. What's home anymore?

She wasn't sure she ever knew. It hadn't been the trailer she'd grown up in. It hadn't even been the Knight house, no matter how much she'd loved it. She'd been too afraid, always, to believe in home. A little too afraid to believe in a future—there, with Cody, with anyone or anything. She'd taken everything one day at a time—always so cognizant of how it could be lost.

Or that home was not for her.

And here she was, with so much to lose, every day. Every breath. She had lost these seven years with him. Because she hadn't told him.

She stood by that decision. Neither of them had been ready for the threat of Ace back then. Not really.

But things were different. They were older. They'd weathered storms, and even a small taste of parenthood together for the last few days. Maybe seven years ago had been the time for caution.

And maybe now, with everything falling around them, but with their family sweeping it all up and stitching it together to protect them, out of love, out of duty.

Maybe now was the time to forget caution. Who knew what tomorrow would bring.

"There was no one else. There's been…nothing else. My life stopped in that moment. A new life was born with Brianna, a new humbling, blinding love. But when your life is changed like that, taken over like that, it's like… I don't know what I'm saying. I don't know what I'm trying to say. It's always been you." She leaned forward, sliding her hands slowly over his, then up his arms. "That hasn't changed. I stopped thinking it could, or even should. It is what it is."

"You still love me." He sounded so shell-shocked. Beyond disbelief, as if he'd been thrust into a new kind of blindness. "We were…young."

"And dumb. So, so dumb. I don't think being young matters. I felt what I felt—I didn't know how precious that was, or how hard it could be. I didn't even know how hard *life* could be then, and it wasn't like I'd had such an easy life. I don't think age changes love. It just changes how you deal with it."

His face was tilted toward hers, but he couldn't see. Because he would do whatever it took to save Brianna. Just like she would—and she had the bullet wound to prove it.

"Cody." She cupped his cheek with one hand, studying his face. Bruised. Scratched. Bandaged.

Yes, she had always loved him—which made her think she always would—but more than that, here was a man who'd lay down his own life, not just to protect her, but to protect anyone he loved—most especially his daughter.

He shook his head against her hand, though she refused to take it away.

"Maybe you don't know the man I've become," he said, his voice hoarse. "What I did with the North Star group..."

"Cody, I've killed two men in the span of a week to save my daughter. Killed. Ended lives. I don't know how I did it. I never thought I would." She used her other hand to hold his face in place. She knew he couldn't see her, but maybe he could feel what she meant if she held on. "It hasn't changed us because we were *born* survivors. We have had to do what needed to be done ever since our doomed parents brought us into the world. So, no, these seven years haven't changed who we are. And as long as Ace has a hold over us, we can't change. We're stuck here."

"I should have killed him."

He said it with such disgust she could only feel sympathy for him, and not wish so much he had. "Maybe that *would* have changed you, Cody. And for whatever reason you didn't, or couldn't. There's no blame for that."

"I've got plenty."

Since she could see the misery on him, the guilt, and she understood that he couldn't end Ace's life, even when he'd wanted to, she brushed her mouth against his again. "I don't," she said against his mouth.

CODY DIDN'T KNOW what they were doing—what Nina, specifically, was doing. Talking about love and guilt and all manner of things that didn't work to keep their daughter safe. Which was all he wanted to do.

Liar.

Something about the way she'd said *survivors*, the way she put the two of them on the same plane as such, the way she laid everything out and it somehow made sense.

They hadn't changed. Love still wound around them, strong and true. Love pulsed here in this cabin, just as it had when he'd seen her being lifted into that ambulance.

Because he'd always known it was his job to survive, and so had she. They would do whatever it took—to survive, to protect.

Would they do whatever it took to love?

Maybe he'd blame all the emotions on being blind and walk away. Or ask to be led away since he wasn't oriented enough in the room to know which way was which.

But Nina's mouth was soft and gentle and it undid him, no matter how he tried to harden himself against it. Nothing had been soft and gentle for seven years, since she'd cut things off. He'd told himself he hadn't missed it. The Wyatts didn't do soft and gentle, and God knew North Star really didn't.

But the longing of someone putting their arms around him, taking some care with how they touched him—it undid everything. He couldn't think past Nina. Couldn't worry that he was the reason they were here, and Brianna wasn't. He couldn't wallow in all that guilt and pain and the horrible, horrible impotence at not being able to end Ace.

Even when he'd had the chance.

Except that reminder pulled him out of the little dream her kiss could provide. He hadn't done what he could to protect Brianna or Nina—even if he hadn't known what would happen at the time.

He eased his mouth away from hers. "Nina. What is this?" He found himself trying to study her face, still oddly confused at the fact he couldn't see. But that persistent gray shadow was all that was in front of him.

Her hands still held his face, her fingers tracing his jaw and the corners of his mouth. "I don't really know. What feels right, I guess. We lost…seven years. Even if we had to, they're lost. But this moment isn't."

She kissed him again, and it turned out kissing her back was one of the few things he was capable of doing easily even without his sight. The sense that he wasn't completely helpless was a comfort. Just like she was.

And no, she hadn't changed. She felt and tasted exactly the same—the softness of her mouth a ghost that had haunted him all this time.

Maybe it had been some kind of subconscious penance to refrain from being with anyone else, and if it had been, didn't he deserve what she so willingly offered?

It was a kiss, and it was comfort they could give each other. A distraction while they waited. It wasn't wrong.

"Make love to me, Cody," she whispered against his mouth.

He wanted to, his body pulsed with the need to have her—and a heart he didn't want to admit was so soft desperately wanted to be with her again. "I... I can't see." A travesty to have her back, even if it wouldn't last, and not be able to see anything.

Still she tugged him to his feet as she chuckled. "Last time I checked eyes weren't a necessary body part for this."

He stood—off-kilter not just because of his lack of sight as she led him forward, but because for all the talk about not changing—she had, in some ways. Maybe not *who* she was, but what she was willing to do and reach for.

Maybe she was nervous and he just couldn't see it, but he wasn't getting the feeling she was unsure or timid. She led him somewhere, and he'd follow her anywhere.

"I always wanted to lead." She put gentle pressure on his shoulders until he sat on the edge of what turned out to be the bed. He scooted himself back, curious how far she would take this.

"So, why didn't you? I probably would have been rather amenable to the idea."

She laughed again, and the sound eased the black tension inside of him. She'd always been able to do that. Soothe, without even trying. She made him believe there was good, light, hope.

Then. Now.

"I didn't know *how* to lead back then. I can't say I'm glad for the past seven years, that we were apart when we didn't have to be. I can't say I'm in any way grateful for what Ace put me—*us* through. But it gave me something I didn't have before, and probably never would have found."

"What?"

She slid over him—a soft, enticing weight as she straddled him. "Courage. Strength."

"You were always brave." He found her hips with his hands. "You were always strong. You just hid it."

She paused above him, but he didn't. He let his hands roam. Had he ever taken his time with her? They'd been teenagers, forever in a rush toward that magic adulthood when things would feel settled, make sense.

What a joke.

But maybe that just meant it would never feel that way, and for once in his life he had to hold on to the now and enjoy it, believe in it.

He slid his hands up her sides, gentling as he felt the bandage under her shirt. "We're pretty banged up."

Fingers traced the bandage on his face.

"Weren't we always?" she whispered, before kissing him as if the admission they'd been bruised and broken internally all those years ago was too much to bear, even after they'd borne so much these past few years.

"I love you," she murmured against his mouth, her body moving against his in blissful agony.

He knew he didn't deserve that—her love, or this, but the same love was inside him, and they had lost so much time. "I love you too."

Chapter Sixteen

Nina woke up to a throbbing in her side and the feeling that she'd actually slept for more than a few fretful hours. The bed was warm and aside from the pain she was getting used to as being just an everyday part of life, she felt surprisingly good.

If it was a nice day, she and Brianna could...

Reality crashed down not just as she remembered she was in a strange cabin far away from Brianna, but as she realized she was naked.

And so was the man next to her.

She couldn't roll over on her side, because it would hurt, but she turned her head to study Cody.

He was still fast asleep, one arm thrown above his head showing off the impressive muscle of his bicep. At some point between *then* and *now* he'd gotten the tattoo he'd always talked about—the cattle brand Grandma Pauline used at the ranch. *A P* and an *R* intertwined, because until Cody's mother had broken the tradition, everyone in the Reaves family had been given the initials *P* and *R*.

Nina had always loved the story. Grandma Pauline

bucking societal convention and refusing to take her husband's name, refusing to act as though he ran the ranch when it was *hers*. Nina had always been fascinated by the man she'd never met who'd agreed to it—purely out of love.

They'd named their only daughter Patricia Reaves-Henderson. She'd broken Grandma Pauline's heart by refusing to use the Reaves and going only by Henderson, by refusing to give the name to any of her children.

By loving a madman.

Nina sighed. So many sad stories in the world and she was in the midst of her own, but it didn't feel sad with Cody next to her. It felt like hope. Life was hard, but there were good things to reach for, hold on to.

Good things to fight for.

The room was dim and Nina realized they'd completely screwed up their sleep schedule and spent most of the day asleep.

The sound of a phone going off in the midst of sleepy silence had Nina jolting and Cody's arm flashing out grasping for the phone. But his instincts were off as he pawed through nothing but air.

Nina's heart twisted as she reached over him to the nightstand where his phone vibrated. She took his hand and placed the phone into his palm, sliding her finger across the screen to answer the call for him.

"Hello," Cody muttered, voice irritated and sleep rasped. Then for the next several minutes he didn't speak as whoever had called him spoke, the volume too low for Nina to make out any of the words.

Cody kept his expression perfectly neutral. She

wanted to touch him, stroke away some of that iron tension inside of him, but she was too afraid of whatever news he was getting.

"All right. Tomorrow then," he said, not giving away if *tomorrow* was good or bad. He held the phone to her and she ended the call for him, then set the cell on the nightstand.

He let out a breath. "They've been busy." He turned his face toward her. Then he frowned, whether something new occurred to him or…

"Can you see?"

He blinked a few times and shook his head, making hope launch through her like a spring.

"No," he said. "But it's…something is different. Lighter, maybe."

"Is that good?"

"I don't… I really don't know."

Nina would pray that it was. "Who was on the phone?"

"Brady. Tuck's got a tail every day, so he's going to be in charge of making it look like he's bringing Brianna to us."

"Won't he be in danger, like we were, of someone trying to attack him? Especially if they think he has Brianna."

"They've got a plan for that. They've got a plan for everything." He didn't sound happy about it. He sounded frustrated.

Nina reached out, rubbed her hand against his arm. "You feel…superfluous?"

He shrugged, but it was an irritable move masquerading as ambivalence. "I am superfluous. We wait. They move. The end." He moved restlessly, inching his way out of bed as he painstakingly felt around for furniture to guide him.

"Let me help you."

"I don't need help for every damn thing," he replied, inching his way down the bed. And he could probably make it out of the room all right, but he was missing a particularly important aspect of getting out of bed.

"You're going to walk around naked all day?"

His scowl deepened and he said nothing.

"I wouldn't complain if you did."

That *almost* got a smile out of him.

"Let me make you some break… Well, I think it's past dinnertime. I'm not sure what you'd call this meal. Postsex sustenance, I guess."

"Stop trying to make me laugh," Cody grumbled.

She slipped on her clothes before going around to his side of the bed. She took his hand.

"Why? You probably need a laugh." She picked up his discarded clothes and helped him into them.

"You've had plenty of laughs these past seven years?" he returned.

"I've tried. For Brianna. We both know bad things happen, terrible things really. We were born knowing that, right? So yeah, I had to figure out how to laugh in spite of it. For Brianna." She placed her hands on his shoulders and brushed her mouth against his. "So, I'll do the same for you."

With only a little fumbling his hands closed over her elbows. Though she knew he couldn't see her, he stared hard at her as if he could. Maybe his sight was coming back—whatever injury was healing and… Maybe this would all be okay.

Hoping for okay seemed so dangerous. Could Cody really get his sight back, could they be some kind of family, without the threat of Ace? Ever?

It was too much to hope for, but all that hope filled her up until she couldn't breathe. It didn't smother the fear inside of her, but it tried.

"Come on. We need to eat something," she said, her voice tight with all those emotions swirling around inside of her.

Still he stared or whatever it was he was doing, holding her in place. It made her heart beat too hard and her pulse scramble for purchase. What was going on in that head of his?

He opened his mouth as if to say something, something serious and important and she held her breath.

Which allowed her to hear a muffled sound that came from outside. Cody frowned, inclining his head where the sound had come from.

Before Nina could ask what he thought it was, or even make a move to look, Cody's phone beeped.

"Get my phone, Nina," he said with a gravity that had her jumping to do just that without asking why.

"There's a gray box, but it's blank."

"Tap it." He talked her through opening some app that made no sense to her, but once he had walked her through it, four squares appeared on the phone screen. Clearly they were video feeds from some kind of surveillance camera.

"What do you see?" Cody demanded.

Nina shook her head trying to make sense of the boxes. They were black-and-white and she could make out trees on one. She didn't remember there being very many trees around the cabin when they'd walked up. Maybe in the back there'd been a cluster? But the memory was hazy because she'd been so focused on Cody and getting to the cabin and help.

"I don't see anything that makes any sense," she finally said as she could sense Cody growing more and more impatient. "Four squares. One has trees, the rest just look gray."

"Ironic," Cody muttered. "Watch the screen."

"What am I looking…" She trailed off as a shadow appeared on the screen. She couldn't make it out, but she could tell something was moving just out of sight of the camera.

"What is it?"

"I don't know. I just could tell something is moving out there, but it's not on the screen. Where are these cameras pointed?"

"You've got four quadrants. A, front. B, left side. C, right side. D, back. Where was the shadow?"

"D."

"That's back. Which area is the shadow in?"

"I… I don't understand all this."

"North, east, west or south, Nina?"

"I don't know!"

"Give me your hand," he ordered.

She wanted to be petulant and refuse—he couldn't see her after all, so he couldn't *make* her. But there was a shadow, and a noise, and a million other fears pounding through her.

She slid her hand into his. He gripped her hand, pulled her toward him, his other hand finding her other arm. His palms moved up until he gripped her shoulders and then he rested his forehead against hers.

"We're okay. I'm frustrated because I can't see. Not at you. Okay?"

She nodded, even if he couldn't see the movement, he could feel it.

"Just describe to me everything you see, and if I snap about something just remember you can take it out on me later if it makes you feel better."

"Did you just make a joke?" She was incredulous, not because of the timing—God knew you had to laugh even in awful times or you never would—but because *he* of all people was joking. Period. Let alone about sex.

"I don't want to add to this…" He made a vague motion with his hands. "I don't want to be a jerk, but I can't see and I'm frustrated so I probably will be. The situation is bad enough without me adding to it, so I'm trying to rein it in. This is my—"

"It isn't your fault. If it was your fault you'd be purposefully hurting me and Brianna and you're trying to save us from the man whose fault it is," she returned, gripping his arm in turn even as he still held her shoulders.

"He's part of me, Nina. I can't escape that."

"Of course you can. If I believed that, I'd have to believe my addict, negligent parents were a part of me I'm helpless to resist, and I've *never* been helpless."

He shook his head, whether to argue or in exasperation that she had an iron-tight argument, she didn't know.

"We can talk blame later. Explain the shadow."

NINA EXPLAINED WHAT she'd seen on the monitors. Cody bit back his impatience with how hard it was to understand what she'd seen when he couldn't see.

He couldn't let himself hope that the fact he seemed to make out some light and some shadow now pointed to the fact he might be healing, the fact he might heal. Because he could just as easily be stuck in this place forever.

And now was not the time to deal with either scenario.

"Do you think someone is out there?"

Cody considered. "Maybe. There are blind spots on the cameras. If someone is out there they don't want us to know and they know how to avoid detection." His father's men hadn't been that smart before now.

At least the men he could get. Cody had to wonder at that. The Sons were a well-oiled machine. Sure, Ace had lost some of his best men in the explosion a few months ago—including his right-hand man. In fact, the death toll included many of the Sons highest-ranking members.

Who had stepped into that power vacuum? Could it be someone who was happy Ace was in jail?

Was it possible Ace had *some* reach from prison, but not a particularly large span because the Sons had gone in a different direction?

He and his brothers had been so focused on Ace in particular, had they considered that Ace might not have the Sons full support now that he was behind bars?

Maybe it had taken him time, or his messenger time, to get someone worth a darn.

And maybe they were here *now*, which would be the problem at hand he needed to focus on. Not what-ifs about the Sons.

"So what do we do? I should call Jamison. I should—"

"We're not calling anyone."

"Cody. Teamwork. We have to be a team. We have to be. For Brianna."

He had been a part of a team for years, but that wasn't what she meant. She said *team* and what she really meant was *family*.

He'd kept himself isolated from his family until two months ago. Visiting infrequently at best, convinced it was necessary to remain secretive about his work with North Star. That had been part of it, but much like why nothing had ever happened with Shay, there was more to it.

He hadn't wanted to depend on anyone. Hadn't wanted to be the littlest Wyatt. He'd wanted to do something on his *own*—for pride and whatever else.

But now he had a daughter, and his pride would have to be swallowed.

"All right. I still want to try and handle this ourselves, but we'll let Jamison know we've got a visitor."

"Or visitors, plural," Nina pointed out.

"Yeah, well. I'll call Jamison. I need you to get the weapons." He explained to Nina where she would find them and how to unlock them. She connected with Jamison's name in his phone for him and he held the cell to his ear as he listened to Nina retreat to where the weapons were hidden.

"Cody."

"J. We think we've got a visitor." He didn't mention there might be more than one. "I don't think we'll need help, but I wanted to let you know."

"But you might need help."

"We can't afford to mess up the plan."

"I'll tell you what we can afford."

"No. You won't. This is my kid at stake. My..." He didn't know what to call Nina, so he didn't finish that sentence. "I call the shots."

"You can't see."

"Everyone keeps reminding me of that as if I don't know very well what I can't do. I've still got a brain."

"A stubborn one."

"Yeah, well, welcome to life with the Wyatts, Jamison. I want to try to capture him and get him to talk."

"How on earth do you think—"

"Have you noticed? How sloppy this barrage of Ace's men are? They're making mistake after mistake. Have you thought about what that could mean?"

There was silence on the other end of the line for a while, so Cody kept talking. "We don't have time to look into it right this second, but it's something to start looking into when we can. It's very possible Ace doesn't have the power we think he does."

"Cody..."

"I'll check in every thirty minutes or so. Don't send anyone out unless I don't check in."

"Cody. That's—"

"It could be a trap, or worse, a distraction. Give me time to handle this. Give *us* time to handle it."

"Twenty minutes. A check-in every twenty minutes," Jamison said, his voice hard, which meant he didn't exactly approve, but he'd go along with it because in the end, Jamison trusted all of them.

Cody had to wonder why. After Dev nearly getting himself killed, Cody couldn't *fathom* why.

But he'd take it. "Fine. Twenty. Is… Brianna close by?"

"Hold on."

It took a few seconds before a young girl's voice filled his ear. "Daddy?"

It was amazing, the fierce sweep of love and longing that swept through him. He'd known her for a few days, and yet her voice steadied him, strengthened him. "Hi, Brianna. Everything going okay at the ranch?"

"Yeah, I guess. I miss Mom."

"I bet you do. Here, I'll have you talk to her in a second, okay?" He could hear Nina approaching. "Are you wearing the necklace I gave you?" he asked quietly into the receiver.

"Uh-huh. Gigi wants one too. Can you make her one?"

"Sure. When I get back. Here's Mom." He held out the phone in the general direction he thought Nina was.

Her fingers brushed his as she took the phone from him. "Brianna?" There was a pause, the faint sound of a sob being swallowed. "Uh-huh. I miss you, baby. I'll be home as soon as I can, okay? Okay. I love you, baby. I love you." Another pause, and then the croak of a goodbye.

"Come here."

He'd barely gotten the words out when Nina filled his arms. He held her tight and she held him back just as strong. She didn't make much noise, but he knew she was crying into his shoulder.

"I just miss her. I can handle it when I don't hear her voice, but..."

"I know. I know." He pulled her back, trying to squint himself into being able to see her face, but it was all still shadows. "So, let's see if we can get back to her sooner rather than later."

Chapter Seventeen

Nina explained the guns she'd found to Cody, and he seemed to file the information away. Then she watched the security footage for a while. No more shadows or hints at anything out there.

It was worse, somehow, the nonthreat after a threat that had never materialized. Worse, with Brianna's voice echoing around in her head from that too-brief phone call. She wanted to be back on the ranch, curled up with Brianna on the couch, reading a book or even watching one of the obnoxious kids shows she loved. Nina wanted her daughter.

And, if she was honest with herself, she wanted to know if anything that had happened with Cody was actually real. Or if it was just the dregs of the past and this whole awful situation.

She knew she loved him still. She had no doubts about her feelings… She frowned over that. If she didn't doubt her own, was it fair to doubt his?

"It could have just been a scouting mission," Cody said into the oppressive silence when still nothing appeared on the screen. They'd been whiling away *hours*.

"What would that entail?"

"See what we've got here and determine what they'd need to successfully breach and attack. Go back and plan, gather, attack later."

It was an awful thought. He no doubt knew what he was talking about, but to wait here patiently while they planned an attack had her pulse hammering in her neck, panic and fear twining deep inside of her gut.

"The problem is," Cody continued, his eyes cast toward his folded hands on the table. "I'm not sure about the endgame. These men who've come after us have been careless. As if they don't care whether we live or die."

"I'm sure they don't."

"That doesn't read as Ace's MO. He wants me alive, so I can suffer. He might want you dead, but it'd be in a way that would make me suffer the most."

"I love being the pawn in some psycho's mind game," she muttered, that edgy feeling after adrenaline wore off making her particularly irritable.

The timer went off and she sent the all clear text to Jamison. It had been hours, so it was just rote now: Set alarm again. Text Jamison 'AC' for all clear, then sit and wait and wait and wait.

"I know this is hard," Cody said after she hit Send. "Waiting is the hardest part. It's a mental game. You have to be tougher than the wait."

"Well, I'm not."

"You are," Cody returned. He held his hand out and she slid hers into it. He gave it a squeeze. "I think you're tougher than anyone has ever given you credit for."

She wanted to cry because she'd had to be tough for seven years without one person telling her she was doing a good job at it, and to have some kind of reassurance, someone believing in her, it mattered. But there was no time for more crying. There was only getting out of this. "How long do we wait?"

"Not much longer. It's possible whoever you saw is already gone. That'd be the smart thing. But these men Ace has had after us… They haven't acted in a way that denotes much intelligence."

"You think he's still out there." The thought gave her a cold shudder.

"I think it's possible there's someone waiting. Setting a trap, maybe. If they have any inclination Brady might come back, or someone else is going to…well, they have a lot of options."

Too many. Too many for them to sit around waiting, that she understood. But he *was* waiting, not acting. He wasn't bringing his brothers into it, and it dawned on her now that it was because he was worried they'd be ambushed.

So, he was waiting. But for what? She studied him, his eyes unseeing, his hands folded so tightly together his knuckles were white. He didn't want to wait. He *had* to wait. "What would you do if you could see?" she demanded.

He shook his head. "It doesn't matter."

But it did. He was holding back because he couldn't

see, and because whatever *he* would do if he had his sight, he didn't trust *her* to do. "Tell me."

"I've been trained to neutralize threats, Nina. Take down crowds of men with lethal weapons. I have been trained to deal with all these kinds of situations, these kinds of men."

"Yes, and while you were being trained, I actually dealt with these kinds of situations, these kinds of men. For our daughter. So, you will tell me. What would you do if you could see?"

His jaw worked, and when he spoke it was pained. "I can't risk anything happening to you."

She wanted to be touched, and she supposed somewhere under the fear and panic she was. But there was too much else going on to spend time on it. "We have to risk *something*. Or we'll never get anywhere. We'll sit here and wait for them to finally rub two brain cells together. If you don't tell me what you would do in this situation with full sight, I will make my own plan, and enact it on my own."

He stood abruptly, then seemed to remember he had nowhere to go without risking running into something or tripping and falling. He balled his hands into fists, but he breathed slow and calm.

"If I could see, I would put to use the many skills I've been taught and slip outside, sneak up to wherever he's hiding—if he is in fact still out there—and I would either fight or threaten him into submission, then bring him in here and demand answers."

Nina thought about it. She could maybe threaten, but she was no expert with a gun and surely the man out there would be. Cody could no doubt overpower someone. Her? Not so much.

So, maybe it was a mistake to expect she could think and act like Cody. She'd saved Brianna. Ace had sent someone to kill her and she'd fought him off. She'd survived.

So, what would she do if she was here, with Brianna? What steps would she have taken to keep her daughter safe?

"If we can't fight them, we can run from them."

"I'm blind. Both of us are banged up from the crash. Running isn't an option, and it doesn't solve anything."

"If we get far enough away, the injuries don't matter. They will keep watching the cabin, hatching their plans, and we'll be long gone."

"And then what?"

Then what? When it had been just her and Brianna, the "then what" had been disappearing and rebuilding a new life. But there was no rebuilding now. There was only keeping Ace behind bars.

And she had help. Regardless of sight, she had Cody. All the Wyatt boys. Her sisters. Duke. She had everyone.

"We get out of here, and then *we* set the trap."

NINA OUTLINED HER PLAN. It clashed with his, which was to wait until dark and then do a little explosives work. But with his sight issues that would be even trickier than he and Nina sneaking out of here.

Cody was starting to see shadows more clearly. He still couldn't see, but he was almost certain he could tell where light was shining from. He hoped it was a positive sign, but since he didn't know for sure, he didn't tell Nina.

"It's a better plan," Nina said as she finished.

"Define *better*."

"Four against one instead of two against one."

"You're assuming there's only one, Nina. That's a dangerous assumption."

"Everything we do is a dangerous assumption, Cody," she returned, irritation straining her voice. "And your plan, if you could see, would be to go out there assuming there's only one you could somehow capture."

"Not necessarily."

Though he couldn't see her roll her eyes, he got the distinct impression that's just what she did.

"Set aside the fact you want to do this on your own. Set aside the fact you want to be in control. Think of my plan from all your angles, and then, if you still don't agree, come up with a better one."

If she hadn't pegged him so dead-on, he might have smiled at the demand in her voice. But the way she picked apart all his trepidation over her plan, made it about his own stupid feelings that didn't matter... Well, it scraped.

And it was exactly what he had to do.

Truth was, if he had a better plan he would have thought of it by now. Waiting was dangerous. It gave whoever was after them too much time to plan, and with time and planning came preparation—which led to an alarming lack of mistakes.

These men after them had made a lot of mistakes

so far. Cody had to keep the momentum going in his and Nina's favor.

"We can't head toward the ranch. It opens up Duke and the others too much, and despite my precautions, puts Brianna in the crosshairs."

"Does North Star have some other kind of place like this?"

"Not for me to use." He could probably finagle it, but he'd likely get Shay kicked out once and for all, and that wasn't his place.

"Let me see that map we used to get here."

He got out his phone and walked her through finding it. There weren't the normal map markers, and her explanation of directions and the markers on the map weren't exactly clear. It took longer than it should have to give him an idea of where they were.

"We're close to the National Park," he said, mulling it over and hoping he'd understood her verbal explanations. "Felicity knows the park better than anyone."

"I don't want to drag her into this."

"She's already dragged, Nina."

"No, she isn't. The only time I've seen Felicity since I've been back was our one whole-families meeting. She didn't even speak to me."

"That doesn't mean Ace won't eventually go after what's yours. His focus is on me, but if you piss him off enough, it could be on you. Which would then extend beyond just Brianna and yourself to Duke and the girls."

For once, he was glad he couldn't see. He didn't want to have to witness what he could already imagine—the color draining from her face, maybe a little horror. She'd never fully understood what getting herself mixed up with him meant.

He supposed none of them had—always thinking they could stay one step ahead. Even after Dev's run-in, Cody had been sure he only needed the *means* to take down Ace. And that was what North Star had been for.

And still he was here. Right here in this awful situation that felt harder and harder to win.

"So, we, what? Hike to the Badlands?"

"More or less. Felicity can give us a clue where to go, and she can either get help to us or be the help to us without drawing much attention. Even if they're following Duke or the girls, they'll get bored real quick trying to traipse around the Badlands after Felicity when it will look like she's just doing her job as a ranger. She's our best bet for help without detection."

"You should be the one to call her. She won't speak with me."

"You underestimate what Felicity would do to help you, Nina. No matter what kind of hurts are running through, they all have your back. They came and took care of our little girl."

He heard her suck in a shuddery breath, but the one she blew out after it was even. "I still think you should call her. You understand the map better. I'll…pack us up with whatever I can find."

"We'll need dark, so you've got time, but we can get a good start. I'll call, you pack. You'll have to carry some guns, supplies. You'll have to study the map and know where you're going. Everything is up to you leading a blind man."

"Not all that different than carrying around a baby, Cody."

"I'm heavier."

"So make sure I don't need to carry you."

She was trying to make light of the situation, feel in control of it, and it fully dawned on him how often she'd been in this exact spot—but alone and with their daughter depending on her.

It awed him—she *awed* him—and some of the anxiety at letting her lead smoothed out. Because she'd kept their daughter safe and alive for *years*.

And what had he done but fail at getting rid of Ace completely?

He wanted to fix that, and maybe he'd get the chance yet, but for now he was still blind and he had to rely on her. Hopefully, he'd get the chance to return the favor.

He held out his phone in the direction he figured she was. "Dial Felicity for me?"

She didn't take it from him immediately, and he got the sense—both in listening to her move and the shadows he seemed to be picking up—she was moving toward him, phone ignored.

She pressed her lips to his, featherlight and sweet, but with a heft to it. "Cody. When this is over—"

He didn't know where she was going with that, had a bad feeling it was something like letting him down easy. Sleeping together had been a one-off, born of panic and fear. She didn't want him to get ideas. "One step at a time."

"When this is over," she repeated, more forcefully. "I need to know Brianna and I have a place in your life. I know she does. I *know* she does. But I need a place there too."

The thing about being blind in a dangerous situation that threatened the life of his daughter and the one woman he'd ever loved was that it stripped all the mental gymnastics he would have done otherwise. He couldn't sit here and worry about if they were the same people, if he could forgive her keeping Brianna from him, if any good thing in life would ever last for him with Ace Wyatt's blood running through his veins— because in the here and now it mattered not at all. Only life mattered. "There's no *place* for you two, Nina. You're both my life."

The phone slipped out of his hand, then back in. "There," she said, her voice oddly calm and solid. "I'll go pack."

Chapter Eighteen

They waited for dark like Cody had suggested. Cody wore the biggest pack, but since she was the one who could see, she needed to be the one with easy access to light and weapons. She had a smaller pack strapped onto her back, a gun holstered to her side and a headband with a light on it on her forehead.

Cody had taken her through how to use the gun, but there'd been no place or opportunity to actually practice. She prayed to God she wouldn't have to use it. Maybe she'd been able to take out the last guy, but that had been in broad daylight.

They had a plan to sneak out the side window—betting that even if there was more than one person out here, they were looking at the exits—not including windows.

They'd had an argument about who would go first. Cody couldn't seem to get it through his head that not being able to see meant he couldn't be the first into danger anymore.

But what impressed her, once she got past her irritation, was that he was trying. He had to be reminded he wasn't Mr. Call-the-Shots, but he'd swallow down that silly pride or whatever it was that made him determined to be in charge, and try to give her room to lead.

Try being the operative word, but not all men would. Especially men like Cody—trained in this kind of thing. He'd spent years with some mysterious group trying to take down one of the most notorious biker gangs in North America. He *knew* what he was doing—he just couldn't enact it.

Meanwhile she was nobody. She could remind herself all she wanted that she'd kept Brianna safe for almost seven years, but as she slid out of the window, doing everything in her power to be stealthy and quiet, the backpack caught on the window and then she banged her knee on the side of the cabin. She held still, half hanging out of the window, holding her breath and listening for sounds of someone coming.

She could hear the sound of an engine, maybe even the faint strains of music. She looked up at the window where Cody was standing. "Are they...listening to music?" she whispered.

"Probably trying to stay awake. Which makes me think there's only one, and he's watching the door. Keep moving."

Nina nodded and took the short jump to the ground. Even without his sight, Cody managed to make climbing out of a window look graceful and easy.

They moved straight back, as they'd planned. They needed to get far enough away that turning on a flashlight didn't give them away. Nina had to admit the moron with the running engine and music playing didn't strike her as the type who'd notice a light *behind* the cabin.

Still, she stuck to the plan. Move forward in a straight line. Wait for Cody, who claimed he had some inner sense of how far they'd gone, to give her the signal.

So she walked, picking her way through the dark as she led Cody. She heard the night go strangely still and Nina paused.

"He cut the engine. Keep moving," Cody whispered. "No lights."

She did so, but something in the air changed and she looked back over her shoulder and stopped dead.

"What is it?" Cody demanded, his body tense and ready to fight no matter that he couldn't see.

"The lights in the cabin just went on," Nina whispered, watching the glow spread—one window, then two, then the window they'd crawled out of.

"It's okay. Keep moving. It'll take him time."

Not enough time, Nina thought, but she swallowed at the panic in her throat and wrenched her gaze away from the light and back to the dark. She needed a minute for her eyes to readjust to the complete dark before she could move forward again.

They walked, on and on. She tried to avoid it, but every once in a while she looked back. The cabin's lights were almost completely gone now, but a new light had joined them. Headlights pointed in the exact direction they'd gone.

"Keep going. Just keep going," Cody urged.

Then she saw a new swath of light moving. A flash-light.

"He's following us."

"Let him."

"We could double back. Leave him to get lost. If he's stupid, he'd get lost out here, surely."

"If he's following us, he won't get lost. He'll just double back too and we're where we started. He might be alone now, but if he's following, he's not *acting* alone. We have to stick to the plan."

"He could—"

"Stick to the plan, Nina. Your plan, remember? Think about what you'd do if you had Brianna."

She'd keep moving. It would be the only choice. She wouldn't like keeping going with someone following, but she'd do it.

So she did.

Then there was the other element of danger that formative years on an isolated ranch in South Dakota made her all too aware of. She knew what lurked in this kind of night. She knew nature could swallow you whole simply for taking the wrong turn or tripping over the wrong animal.

One scary threat at a time.

She managed to put some distance between them and the moving light, which gave her some hope he wasn't following tracks so much as looking for them.

"Still no light, but let's get the map out," Cody suggested.

Bringing out the phone would put off a small light, but she'd be able to mitigate how brightly it shined.

Cody had showed her how to bring everything up, talked her through how to follow the map—just as he had the first time they'd had to use it. She paused just long enough to grab the phone and bring up the correct app.

Cody held on to her coat so she no longer had to hold his hand. It made it harder to lead him around potential tripping hazards, but aside from a few stumbles he quickly righted himself from, they were doing okay.

They had a hell of a long way to go though.

Nina focused on the end result, just as she would if she was with Brianna. Get to the meeting point Felicity and Cody had agreed upon. That was all she could worry about right now.

Get them to the agreed upon area, then wait till morning. Without their little friend back there catching up and finding them.

She let out a shaky breath, but kept moving. She forced herself to only look back every once in a while, was gratified each time she'd put more space between them and the moving light. She wished they could lose him completely, but she had to follow the map.

They'd initially planned to stop every hour or so, get a drink and a snack, but there'd be no stopping now. Just cold, endless hiking.

Cody fell once, nearly brought her down with him but managed to release her coat just in time. She looked up at where the light was. She could barely see it now, but she could sense he'd stopped too. The light didn't move.

She helped Cody up, one eye on that light. "Maybe we should—"

"Follow the map," Cody interrupted, getting to his feet. "Follow the map, get to the spot. Felicity might not be there yet, but we can hold off whoever this is until she gets there. Then we'll have help. Any help we'd get here is too long off."

He was right, of course, which was irritating. But irritating didn't matter when you were running—or walking quickly—for your life.

By the time she reached where the interactive map told her to stop, there was the faintest hint of light on the horizon. Morning was coming. She didn't think they'd lost their stalker, but she couldn't see his flashlight anymore.

There were signs that they were entering national park land. Not much cover, as the Badlands wasn't known for its forests.

"Now what?" Nina asked, tired and achy and starving.

"Felicity said we should be able to find some shallow caves around here."

"Caves." Nina shuddered. "Great."

"It'll keep us out of sight. We can sit, eat, rest."

Nina hefted out a sigh. "I'll need my flashlight then. I don't see the guy, so it might be safe." She looked at Cody, standing there. It'd be so much easier if she could search for caves without having to maneuver him around the rocky, uneven ground.

"Leave me here."

She frowned at how easily he read her. "I wouldn't leave Brianna here. I thought we were doing—"

"Leave me here, Nina. Find a cave. I'll shout if I get scared."

She nearly snorted. He wouldn't shout, because he wouldn't get scared—even if he should.

"Just go, Nina. I might be blind, but I'm not a small child. Give me *some* credit."

It wasn't about credit, but she didn't have time to argue with him. She'd go search for a place to hide for ten minutes tops, and if she didn't find one she'd come back and get him. But she wouldn't tell him that.

"All right. Stay put. Give some kind of signal if you need me, Cody. Promise me that."

"Sure," he replied.

Because of course him admitting he needed someone was as likely as him admitting he was scared. Wouldn't happen.

"I'll be back," she said, and hoped it would be as easy as that.

CODY HEARD THE APPROACH, knew it wasn't Nina's. He held himself tense, ready, and listened closely to the sounds. Careful but confident, a lighter footfall could be Felicity or someone being careful to sneak up on him.

Cody listened, angled himself toward the noise, and hoped to God Nina was being careful wherever she was.

Though he knew it was likely still dark, he could tell his vision was worse again. Mostly grayness with no sense of light or shapes and his head ached and pounded. But that only served to give him *some* hope.

If when he'd been well rested and calm he'd started to be able to have some concept of light and shadow, he'd been healing and his sight had been coming back. The walk and the handful of stumbles he'd taken had made the healing regress.

But he could heal.

He would heal.

Another set of footsteps approached from behind him, and he could tell those were Nina's. "I think I found—" Nina stopped her whispered sentence on a sharp intake of breath.

"You two look like hell."

It was Felicity's voice and Cody felt a relief so wide and deep he nearly stumbled. "You're early," he managed to rasp. He'd told her to wait. Give it until park hours started and make it look like she was just doing part of her job coming to this isolated area of Badlands National Park.

He hadn't wanted her followed or involved and God only knew what Ace had up his sleeve. But with a man following them and his vision worse, he could only be utterly grateful for Felicity ignoring his orders.

Two sighted women with his instruction against one stalker was far better odds.

"I have a program at nine," she replied, her tone still oddly detached and cool when usually Felicity was timid but sweet. "I couldn't get out of it, and I figured this would take a while." There was a long pause. "God knows I was right. We've still got a way to go on foot. I couldn't take my vehicle back here."

"Someone might have followed us," Nina said, her

voice hesitant and unsure. "This whole way. Someone was following us. I'm not sure we lost him completely."

Cody had almost forgotten that's how she'd been at first, with everyone else. She'd always been fierce and determined with him. Or sad, which was worse than anything. But those initial meetings with Duke and the sisters—she'd had this timidity to her.

Felicity's pause made him wonder if Nina hadn't been closer to the truth on Felicity's feelings regarding Nina, but Felicity was here, to help. That was what mattered right now. Not what they needed to work out about the past.

"Well, then let's get going," Felicity said at length.

"Did you tell anyone?" Cody demanded as he felt Nina's arm twine with his. She urged him to step forward.

Again Felicity's pause was telling.

"I told you not to."

"You did," Felicity agreed. "I'm sorry, I thought it best if someone knew. Not just for you, but for me too."

"They need to protect Brianna."

"I'm sure they'll find a way to do both," Felicity said gently.

Admittedly, if not for her job, Felicity never would have been his first pick for help. She was gentle and shy. Liza and Sarah were all sharp edges, and Nina and Cecilia were wary edges, but Felicity and Rachel were sweet and soft and not fighters of any kind.

But Felicity worked at the park, and that's where they'd been. He really hadn't expected her to go against what he'd told her.

Cody grumbled his displeasure as Nina led him forward. "We can't just walk. He's tracking us at this point. If we just go to your vehicle, he'll see what happened. He'll mark you too."

"And as far as you know he doesn't have a vehicle on hand, so what's it matter?"

"I don't want him making you, Felicity. We've got enough people in danger. I called you as a last resort, and because I'd have the best chance of keeping you the hell out of it."

"None of us are out of it, Cody. Doesn't anyone understand how this all works? We're a family. We take care of one another." There was a fierceness in her voice he hadn't expected, but appreciated in the moment.

Still. "The point isn't what we are, the point is who Ace targets."

"Right now, he's targeting you two."

"And our daughter."

"And your daughter. Don't you trust your family to protect her, Cody?"

He shut his mouth, because there was no good answer for that. He did. But that didn't mean it wasn't terrifying to put his daughter's life in someone else's hands no matter how much he trusted them. Especially when they were up against Ace.

But they'd gotten this far, and Cody continued to believe Ace was incapacitated in *some* way.

Nina stopped abruptly, and neither woman spoke.

"What?"

"Rattlers. We're going to have to backtrack and go around the other side."

Since Cody couldn't see he didn't know what "other side" Felicity was referring to, but Nina turned him around and started leading him again.

Backtracking was no good, rattlers or no. Surely dawn was beginning to streak across the sky and surely their stalker was closing in.

"Look around, Nina," he said in a low voice, hoping Felicity was far enough ahead of them she couldn't hear. "Keep your eyes peeled for our friend."

"I am," Nina returned easily. "Sun's rising. He won't need a flashlight anymore, but the trees and rock formations are still dark. He could easily hide in the shadows."

"I've got binoculars. Do you want to stop behind some cover and check?"

As much as Cody preferred science, reason and technology, sometimes a gut feeling was all a man had, and the way the hairs on the back of his neck stood on end, something was coming.

"Give Felicity a gun, Nina," he ordered, trying to figure out which way the threat was coming from.

"I can't have your gun, Cody. I'm a park ranger. It's illegal to—"

"Take the gun, Felicity. We're going to need it."

Chapter Nineteen

"Let's get situated first," Nina said, nodding toward a rock outcropping that would hopefully hide all three of them.

Felicity moved in first, and without saying anything, Nina helped Cody into the spot before scooting in herself. Tight fit, but they would be mostly hidden from the direction their stalker had been coming from.

She unzipped her pack and handed Felicity one of the guns they'd packed and then the magazine.

"This is illegal," Felicity muttered, though she took the gun and put it together with some ease.

"Write yourself a ticket later," Cody muttered. "You see anything?"

Felicity lifted the binoculars to her eyes. She was quiet and scanning, and Nina had to close her eyes and inwardly count to five to try to find some center of calm. "He's coming. Far-off, but on his way."

"We should just go." She couldn't help saying it. How could they sit here and wait around for a threat to appear when they could be fleeing it? "He doesn't have a vehicle. How is he going to know we got one from a *specific* park ranger?"

"How did Ace know where *you* were?" Cody countered.

She didn't have a good answer for that, so she kept her mouth shut.

"So, what are we going to do, Cody?" Felicity asked.

She wasn't exactly as Nina remembered her. The Felicity she remembered had been shy to the point of running and hiding in her room when the Wyatt boys were around. She'd had a stutter for a while. Nina had always believed Felicity would grow out of that shyness a bit, but figured she'd always be more on the anxious, high-strung side of things.

This Felicity was calm. There was something regal about her, and it wasn't the drab brown park ranger uniform with a badge that gave that aura. It was self-possession and confidence.

"Nina, you remember my idea back at the cabin?" Cody asked, though she knew it wasn't a real question. He was going to lay out this plan like it was what they had to do.

"No," she retorted harshly. Not because she didn't remember, but because there was absolutely no way the three of them were going to endanger themselves to try and capture their stalker.

"The more information we have, the better chance of keeping Ace out of our lives better. Longer."

Which was tempting. She had to get Ace completely and utterly neutralized, though she didn't know how that was going to happen without ending his life.

Which was why this felt like an unnecessary risk. "What about the risks?"

"We mitigate them."

She hated when he responded with those non-answers spoken with such surety and conviction—both things she couldn't muster now. She was exhausted and aching and starving.

"For every moment we spend talking, he's getting closer," Felicity informed them, her binoculars trained somewhere beyond the rock.

"Good. We want him close."

"*You* want him close," Nina returned. "You don't even know he has any connection to Ace. If they're all this bad at coming after us, surely it's because there's some kind of conduit hiring them."

"Yes, and wouldn't it be good to know who that conduit is?"

She couldn't argue with that. Still, this felt like putting their lives in danger for a chance instead of a sure thing.

"I could pick him off. Shoulder or thigh or something," Felicity said, still intent on the binoculars. "Slow him down."

Nina blinked at Felicity. "Could you really?"

Felicity smiled over at Nina a little sheepishly. "A lot happens in seven years, Nina." She turned back to the binoculars. "You'll get caught up."

It was the first encouraging thing one of the sisters aside from Liza had said to her.

"I don't want you to shoot him," Cody said. "Too risky."

"I'm a good shot. Ask Brady."

"Some things haven't changed," Nina muttered, hanging on to that same hero worship in Felicity's voice that had always been there when it came to Brady.

Felicity gave her a wide-eyed *don't you dare* look that reminded Nina of old times so sharply she wanted to cry.

But there still wasn't time for that.

They all swore in an echoing kind of unison, ducking farther behind the rock they were all huddled behind as a gunshot rang out and crashed into the rock in front of them.

Cody's face went grim, icy. "Okay, Felicity, shoot him. Try for the leg. We want him alive and able to talk. But make sure he's stopped."

Felicity handed Nina the binoculars then lifted the gun Nina had handed her earlier. Nina watched in fascination as her shy, nervous sister calmly lifted the gun to rest on the rock. She waited with the rest of her body still hidden behind it before she carefully inched her way back up, clearly testing if their stalker would shoot again.

"Easy," Cody murmured, and Nina supposed it was just a general comment since he couldn't see.

"Distract him, Nina," Cody ordered. "Stick the backpack up or something he'll shoot at or look at, but won't hurt."

Nina scrambled to follow the order, and Cody kept giving clear, precise orders. "He shoots, you shoot, Fee, got it?"

"Yup."

They were so calm, and Nina tried to find her own. She'd run away from men with guns before. She'd saved her daughter—and at least mentally that'd been easier. Because all she'd ever thought was *how do I keep Brianna safe.*

There were too many people, too many layers now. She believed Brianna was safe at the ranch because she had to, but her, Cody and now Felicity were all in danger. Immediate, gunshot danger.

But Cody had given her a job. She shrugged the lighter pack off her back. With shaking limbs she lifted the backpack slowly up so it was visible over the rock. The sound of a gunshot was almost immediate.

"All right," Cody said, each word cold and forceful. "Shoot."

The sound of the gunshot next to him had Cody flinching even though he'd expected it, braced for it. Ordered it, so to speak.

Felicity let out a little *yes*, and he took that as success. "Got a sense of where you hit?"

"Thigh. Fell right down, but he's trying to get back up."

"Nice aim. Okay, let's get him."

"Let's?" Nina demanded. "You can't see."

"I love how you keep reminding me of that, Nina." He stood to his full height, then ducked when a gunshot farther off slammed through the air. Judging by the sound as it impacted the rock not that far from his head, it was way too close.

"He's still got a gun, Cody," Felicity said drily.

"Gee, you don't say."

"You should stay here," Nina said next to him. "You can hardly walk over there *not* being able to see."

"And you two can hardly walk over there getting shot at," he retorted. He thought he'd been handling his loss of sight pretty well, but right about now he would have sold his soul to be able to see and *accomplish* something.

"I can sneak around behind him," Felicity said.

"No," Nina and Cody replied in unison.

Felicity huffed out a breath. "I know the landscape better than either of you—and God knows you can't see, and Nina…"

"I can handle it. I can do it."

Though it went against everything he wanted, Cody knew what had to be done. "You'll both do it."

He'd expected immediate retorts and arguments, but there was nothing but heavy silence in response.

"You hate that I keep reminding you," Nina began softly. "But how can we leave you here when you can't see?"

"I'm the distraction," Cody replied. "It doesn't matter if I can't see if I can distract."

"It does if he gets to you," Felicity pointed out.

"Not if you guys are right behind. Listen, I don't think he'll kill me. Ace wouldn't want him to kill me."

"That doesn't mean he won't. He kind of sucks at his job, if you haven't noticed."

"Unfortunately, we don't know what his job is. Now, you guys have to take off and get behind him. If he starts coming for me, no matter how slowly, you need to get going."

Though he couldn't see, he had no doubt Nina and Felicity were sharing a wordless look as they decided what to do.

He heard shuffling. Then Felicity spoke. "He's up, but he's moving slow. If we hurry, I think we can get around him before he makes it here."

"You have to make sure he doesn't hear you."

"And what are we going to do if we *do* sneak up on him? Tackle him?" Nina demanded.

"Why not?" Felicity replied with a shrug in her voice. "It wouldn't be the first guy I've had to tackle out here."

"Really?" Nina replied, clear awe in her voice, which didn't make any sense to Cody, considering Nina had done way more than tackle a guy.

"Get his gun off of him. And any other weapons he has. Whatever ways you've got. Then we want to know who sent him, how he's getting orders from Ace. Once he's incapacitated enough, someone come back here and get me so I can question him."

There was another silence that Cody had no doubt included silent communication between the women. He couldn't say he trusted them to follow his orders word for word, but he didn't have other choices.

"All right," Felicity said at length. "Nina, follow me."

There was shuffling and rustling and as Cody tilted his head toward it, he realized he could make out shadows again. There was even almost a hint of color when he held his head just so.

Nina's mouth brushed his. "Be careful," she whispered.

He gave a nod, his vision going back to gray then everything too bright so he flinched back. He tried to play it down. "You too."

She didn't move for a second, but she didn't say anything else. Then he could hear them moving out. Situated in rock the way they were, it made an awful lot of noise. Though he imagined a man who'd been shot would make a lot of noise on approach.

He was counting on it anyway.

He felt around for the backpack, made a lot of noise drawing it onto his lap. He blinked three times when he realized he could see the shape of it.

He took a deep breath, willing himself not to get overexcited that his sight might be coming back at the exact right time. He felt around in the pack, because though he could see it he couldn't make out the details of what was inside. That was all shadow. Out of focus.

But he found what he wanted and pulled the sheathed knife out of the pack. He set the pack aside and then moved onto his feet, crouching low. He reached out, felt the cool, jagged rock in front of him, slowly inching up and up until he found the top of the rock.

He held up the tip of the knife, bit by bit, higher and higher, keeping his breathing even so the pounding of his heart didn't interfere with his hearing.

Once he'd extended his arm fully, he moved the knife back and forth, hoping it would catch in the sun.

Because it was daylight. He could *tell* the sun had risen.

Focus.

There was still no response to him holding up the knife, and it made him nervous that he wasn't being the distraction he needed to be. Still, he couldn't stand just yet. He strained to listen over the wind whistling through the canyons.

He thought about banging his knife against the rock, but that would be an obvious attempt for attention. He had to do something that might draw fire without actually getting caught in said fire.

Then Cody heard it. The distinct sound of rubble crumbling under careful pressure. As if someone was climbing up the other side of the rock.

A tough climb with a gunshot wound to the thigh, but when he heard a pained grunt that definitely came from a man, he knew that's exactly who was trying to make the climb anyway.

Cody positioned himself farther back, hoping he was facing the right direction to have a sense of when the man first saw him. He held the knife loosely at his side. If he trusted his sight more he'd try to look for the man, get an advantage and knock him down, but it was too risky.

Besides, Nina and Felicity were supposed to be sneaking up behind the man. They'd have time—and guns—Cody would be fine.

There was a low chuckle, and Cody kept himself still and poised. He couldn't make out an exact outline, but he could sense the position of the man, get a sense of light and shadow. He only needed another sound cue and he could reach out and land a blow.

God, he hoped.

Chapter Twenty

Nina and Felicity didn't talk. Felicity walked at a break-neck speed through rock formations, pausing only when they had to cross fields with no cover. She'd look, then cross at speeds faster than breakneck.

Nina didn't complain, though she was out of breath and had a stitch in her side as she hurried along after Felicity. The longer they left Cody alone, *blind*, the more she worried.

There'd been a sense that maybe he'd been able to see for a moment, but he hadn't said anything. So she hadn't. Besides, even if he did regain his sight it wouldn't just magically appear right when it would come in quite handy.

"Crap," Felicity muttered, coming to a quick stop. She pointed to a ridge. Nina was all turned around after the fast-paced, zigzagging run Felicity had taken her on. In front of them rock and grass stretched out as if fighting each other for purchase, but there was a man climbing up that ridge, and Nina had no doubt it was the outcropping of rock they'd been on the other side of.

The gun the man held in one hand glinted in the ever-increasing sunlight.

"Run," Nina ordered. They both did. Because on the other side of that rock Cody was a sitting duck.

Just as they reached the bottom of the rock the man was scaling, he fell straight back with a howl.

All Nina could do was watch him fall, and wince when his body landed with a thud.

"He's still got the gun," Felicity warned, already leaping forward. Nina did the same even as he brought that arm up, struggling to roll over and point it at them.

They both lunged at the same time, and the weight of two women had no problem knocking the gun out of the man's grasp. It skidded across scrubby grass and rock and Nina sucked in a breath as pain had her seeing stars. But she quickly scrabbled to her feet as Felicity did—though Felicity did it much more gracefully in Nina's estimation.

Since the gun was closest to her, Nina hurried to pick it up. Then looked up at the rock the man had been climbing.

In wordless agreement, Nina handed Felicity the gun, then turned away from her and the moaning and thrashing man. Felicity would handle him while she attempted to climb up and check on Cody.

It was a hard climb, and she was shocked the man had done it with a bullet wound to the leg. Still, despite a few slips and slides she managed to get to the top.

Cody was slinging one of the packs onto his back. He turned slowly, blinked a few times. "Where's Felicity?"

"Can you see?" she breathed.

"Not...exactly. I don't know. It clears up then goes back. Where is he? I assume he's alive from all that racket?"

"He fell. Straight down. Felicity's got the gun on him. How..."

"I hit him. Didn't mean to knock him over, but it'll do. Get me down there."

She shouldered the bag she'd left behind earlier and then took his hand. She looked dubiously down the sharp rock. "We could go around—"

"Quickest way, Nina. Let's end this."

She liked the sound of the word *end* too much not to do her best to help him down the climb. She figured he had to be seeing at least a little bit because he didn't stumble.

They made it to the bottom where Felicity stood over the man, who was still lying on the ground but was mostly still except for the rapid rise and fall of his chest. Felicity had both the gun Nina had handed her earlier and the gun they'd gotten off the stalker pointed at him.

Cody studied him before he said anything, but his gaze wasn't directly on the man—it was a little to the right. So whatever pieces of sight were back, it wasn't total.

"Gotta name?" Cody asked.

The man's moaned response was vulgar.

Cody's response kick to the ribs was vicious—and surprisingly on target for a man with limited sight.

"We could just leave him," Felicity offered casually, studying the man on the ground as if he were an interesting piece of roadkill. "Rattlesnakes. Bobcat. Coyotes. Hell, the elements'll get him before any of the animals start nibbling."

Cody's mouth quirked. "We'd have to tie him down or something though. Just to make sure he couldn't crawl his way out."

"Or you could shoot his other leg," Nina offered.

This time Cody smiled, though it was sharp and feral at the edges. "Bloodthirsty. I like it."

"You think I'll live if I tell you anything?" the man demanded, but his eyes went back and forth between them and then to the harsh surroundings.

"I could make sure you do."

The man snorted. "You don't get in my position and live. So shoot me."

Cody held out a hand and both Nina and Felicity stared at it.

"You can't—"

He sent Nina a glare that had her snapping her mouth shut. On a shrug, Felicity handed one of the guns to Cody. He held it right to the man's skull and Nina sucked in a breath, bracing herself for the sound of a gunshot even as her brain screamed that this couldn't actually be happening.

The man tried to scoot away, eyes widening and sweat popping up on his forehead. "Okay, okay. Wait. Just…wait."

"Name."

His eyes darted around to all three of them, then beyond, as if calculating his chances of survival. He licked his lips.

"How exactly can you make sure… How are you going to protect me? *Why* are you going to?"

"If you give me the information I want, your identity will cease to exist. I'll get you a new one. I don't need your life. We both know you're a low man at best. I don't care about *you*. I care about information."

The man gestured helplessly at where his leg was bleeding pretty profusely.

"You'll get medical attention and a new identity. Or you're dead. So, make a choice."

"I don't know anything. I just get orders and I follow them."

"Who from?"

He looked around again. "I don't have a name."

Cody stepped closer, crouched down, got the gun right up in the guy's face. "I don't have much patience left. You will give me his name. Now. Or…"

"Fine. Andy. Andy Jay."

Nina watched as Cody immediately stood, still with the gun pointed at the man. His expression was rage. "Don't lie to me. Andy Jay is dead."

The man started to shake, held up both hands in supplication. "That's the name I got. That's the only name I ever heard. Andy Jay. I swear it."

Cody didn't lower his gun, and the cold fury in his gaze made Nina shiver. But then something mechanical echoed around them. It was coming from the rocks. She supposed it was Cody's phone, though she would have thought it would be on silent. But the look on his face had her body going cold.

"What is it?"

Cody's expression had changed, turned to that stone that only meant trouble. Deep, horrible trouble. "We have to go. Now."

THERE WAS ONLY one reason his phone would make that sound—especially if it was on silent.

Brianna had pushed her necklace button.

He shoved the gun into Felicity's hand. "Call...one of my brothers." He swore internally. If something was going down at the ranch, they should all be there. "If you don't get anybody, just call the sheriff's department."

"Hey! You said you'd get me a new identity. You said—"

Cody aimed a killing look at the man—what he could make out of his sprawled-out body. He'd been planning on helping the guy, but Cody was almost certain the name he'd been given was bogus. And he was quite certain Brianna was in trouble, so he didn't concern himself with the lowlife who would have happily killed all of them.

"Never trust a Wyatt," he told the guy flatly.

He turned back to the tall, willowy shadow that he knew was Felicity. His brain was scrambling. He couldn't leave her alone with this guy. Sweet, nervous Felicity, who'd handled all of this without even the hint of a qualm.

Maybe she could handle it. She had to. Brianna

was in trouble and that came above everyone else. He looked over at the figure that was Nina. Some of his vision sharpened, and he swore he could make out the bright beacon of blond hair in the sunlight.

He wanted to leave her with Felicity, but he didn't have enough of his sight back to drive. And he knew she wouldn't appreciate being left behind without good reason. Protecting her would not be considered a good enough reason.

"What is it?" she demanded again.

"Trouble at the ranch. We need to—"

"Here," Felicity interrupted. He heard a jangle, got the impression she'd tossed keys that Nina had caught. "Drive my truck. I'll take care of this guy. You guys go. Once you get to the other side of that ridge, there's a trail. You'll catch it and follow it to the trailhead. Once you're there, my truck's in the lot. Should be the only one. I'll handle this here. I've got my phone plus radio if I can't get ahold of who I want to—I can get another ranger out here. You go."

Cody nodded. No time to argue or think of a better plan. He needed to get to Brianna.

Nina's hand curled around his arm and she began to lead him, presumably where Felicity had instructed. He still couldn't see much of the ground except a broad swath of light, with the occasional blip of something he assumed were the rock outcroppings the Badlands were known for.

He wanted to hurry, but hurrying would likely end in him tripping and falling flat on his face, probably bringing Nina with him. No time for falls or stumbles, even if it meant the walk was slow and steady.

He hadn't had time to climb back up and get his phone, so he could only hope to God it had been a mistake, or his brothers were taking care of it. But he couldn't gamble with the time it would have taken to recover the phone and be sure.

The walk seemed to take forever, and even once Nina helped him into Felicity's truck—then climbed in the driver's seat herself—they still had a forty-five-minute drive to the ranch.

But Nina started to drive, and he doubted she was paying much attention to the posted speed limits.

"Who's Andy Jay?" she asked.

Cody shook his head. "He's dead."

"Okay. Who *was* he then?"

"I'm not sure exactly. Part of the Sons. One of Dad's main guys back in the day. I don't particularly remember him, but I know of him from stories. When Brady and Gage escaped to Grandma's… He caught them and let them go instead of bringing them back to Ace. Then he was found dead a few days after Gage and Brady made it to the ranch with Jamison. The twins always blamed themselves. So, that guy's lying about Andy Jay."

Nina was quiet, but he could hear and feel how quickly she was driving. Still, she was calm. Probably because he hadn't mentioned the alarm would have come from Brianna—not one of his brothers.

"If the guy out there with Felicity was part of the

Sons, or involved, he'd know Andy Jay was dead and that you'd know who it was."

"Yeah. Probably Ace trying to twist the knife."

"Or someone purposefully using that name."

Cody shook his head. He couldn't work it out, but he could only think about Brianna. Who was in trouble. "When we get there…" He trailed off, because he didn't know how to broach the subject. His sight was coming back. Not near what he needed though. But he could hardly send Nina into a dangerous situation to yet again handle the saving of their daughter all on her own.

"When we get there what?"

He blew out a breath. "We have to be careful."

"What did that noise mean? It was some kind of signal from the ranch?"

Cody shifted in his seat. He didn't want to lie to her. Even if he'd be in the right, she'd blame him for it. Which struck him as ironic, considering she'd kept Brianna a secret from him.

But a secret was different than a lie. Especially when it involved their daughter's life.

"I don't know what exactly is going on. That sound from my phone just means someone was alerting me to an emergency."

"Help, you mean. Someone at the ranch needs help. They're in danger. And, knowing all they knew about where we were and what we were doing, they still need help from you."

"Presumably."

She didn't say anything to that, but he could sense

the increasing speed of the vehicle. Not being able to see clearly made that a heck of a lot more nerve-racking than it would have been otherwise.

"You can't go careening onto the property. We have to see what we're up against first."

"Our daughter is in that house. Screw what we're up against."

Since he'd felt that echo through him at first, he didn't immediately argue with her. Maybe he should have told her back with Felicity exactly what that sound had meant—because he'd had a chance to walk off his excess anger and fear and find some clearheaded focus.

Whatever was going on at the ranch, they had to be careful. They had to get a sense of it before they ran in guns blazing. Most especially because Brianna was in danger—and any wrong move could risk everything.

Andy Jay. The man was dead—Cody was sure of it. That was how the story went, and he doubted his brothers would beat themselves up over his death without knowing for sure it was him who was dead.

Or had they all been too young to be that cynical?

He had no phone to warn Brady or Gage. No way of finding out what was really going on at the ranch. He wanted to believe Brianna had touched it out of curiosity, or as an accident… But she was too bright, too cognizant of the trouble she'd grown up in to be careless.

Eventually he could feel the truck begin to slow. His vision was still mostly a blur, such a blur he had to close his eyes half the time to ward off dizziness.

"Don't go to the front gate. You remember the side one? Back off Frank's Lick Road. Let's ease in there."

"Too late for that," Nina muttered darkly.

"What do you see?"

He felt her pushing his head down. "Duck."

Chapter Twenty-One

The gunshot shattered the windshield and Nina had to swallow a scream.

She should have slowed down earlier, but she'd been desperate to get to Brianna and then surprised to drive past a very large SUV with two very large men fiddling with something along the fence of Grandma Pauline's property.

When she *had* seen them, it hadn't been much of a surprise to see a gun lift and point in their direction.

Nina peeked up, saw she was careening for a utility pole and jerked the wheel. "Any weak spots on the fence I can bust through?"

"No. We'll have to do it on foot."

"What?" she demanded.

"Stop the truck."

"We can't—"

"Stop the truck," Cody insisted. She thought it had to be insanity. She'd rather bust through the fence with Felicity's truck and worry about the damage later.

But she trusted Cody, so she stopped. "You still got a gun?"

She nodded, patting her side where she'd strapped it back at the cabin what seemed like forever ago. "Yeah."

"You run for the house. I'll go for them."

"You can't see—"

"I can. Good enough anyway. Go!" He started pushing at her and she didn't have time to think. Brianna was in the house. That could be her only thought.

So she got out of the truck and started running. With every step she reminded herself Cody could handle himself. Would handle himself.

The important thing was Brianna.

Damn it, he better come out of this alive or she'd kill him herself.

She ran and ran, ignoring the horrible pain in her side and her struggling breath.

Brianna. Brianna. Get to Brianna.

No one shot at her and she didn't see anyone, though she didn't have time to look around and scan the surroundings. But nothing stood out to her as being off. No other SUVs. No big men in black. Jamison's and Gage's trucks were outside the house in the distance, and Tucker's SUV was parked near the barn.

Maybe those two men had been it. Maybe somebody inside had somehow seen or…

Keep running. Keep breathing.

She continued across the yard, half expecting another gunshot or someone to jump out at her, but no one did.

She made it to the door and burst in, horrified to find it unlocked. Even more horrified to find four men,

Duke and Grandma sitting around the kitchen table. "What on earth are you all doing? Where's Brianna?"

"She's out in the barn with Gigi and Dev," Grandma Pauline returned, rising to her feet. "What's going—"

"Cody's out front. Someone's shooting. Big black SUV, two guys, a few yards before the front gate on the road." She was already running out the door. Maybe Cody was the one in real danger, but she had to be sure that her daughter was safe.

She knew the Wyatt brothers would go help Cody, and she would too as soon as she knew for sure Brianna was fine.

So, she ran for the barn. She skidded to a stop outside the barn when she heard voices. Not ones she recognized. Well, she recognized Dev's voice, but not the other person's.

Heart rioting in her chest, she inched closer and closer, trying to see what was going on. Trying to see where Brianna was.

The barn door was open, but all she could make out was Dev talking to someone. He seemed calm as he came into view. Just standing there, attention on someone out of view, but the closer she got, the more she recognized the banked fury in his voice. He wouldn't talk to the girls like that. Ever.

Trying not to gulp for air, she changed her angle to see where Dev was looking. Sure enough, there was a large man, with a very large gun, pointed right at Dev's chest.

Where was Brianna? And Gigi?

She took a slow, quiet deep breath. Okay. So, it

seemed like there were three men. Six Wyatts, Grandma Pauline and Duke, plus her and Liza—they could take three men. Even ones with big guns.

So she needed to focus on her daughter. Where would Brianna be? Surely Dev would do anything to keep the girls from getting hurt.

She reached for her weapon as she heard soft, careful footsteps behind her. Hand on weapon, ready to draw and shoot, she whirled.

Then scowled at Tucker, who held his hands up, but not without the mocking lift of an eyebrow.

Like any of them had time for *mocking*.

He didn't say anything, only pointed up. She turned back to the barn, didn't see anything, but she wasn't meant to. It was a reminder there was a hayloft. The girls must have hidden.

Relief swamped her, not that it took all the fear away. But the man with the gun must not know where those two precious girls were.

Please God.

She looked at Tucker, seeking some kind of guidance. With two of them, surely they could take out the man in the barn. She didn't see a gun on Tuck, but that didn't mean he didn't have one.

He made hand motions, circling a finger then pointing to the ground. It took a few times through for her to get he was saying he was going to walk around to the other side and she should stay right here.

She nodded, and Tucker began to walk to the back of the barn. There was another door on the other side, but from what Nina could see it didn't look to be open.

But it *was closer* to the ladder that would lead up to the girls.

But how did Tucker know they were up there? He was just making a guess. They could have run. They could be lost in the fields and—

One problem at a time.

She kept her gaze on the man talking to Dev. Actually *at* Dev was a better description since Dev's mouth hadn't moved once. The door on the opposite side of the barn didn't move—so what the hell was Tuck doing over there?

Nina sighed, rolled her shoulders in an attempt to keep her body from going tight after the crash a few days ago plus all this running and hiking and climbing. She couldn't let the tension centering between her shoulder blades keep her from being agile.

Finally Dev spoke, making a gesture toward the house—which was a gesture toward the open door and Nina herself.

Nina froze.

Dev's gaze met hers, and though she thought he hid his surprise at seeing her rather well, the man with the gun trained on Dev began to turn.

Nina didn't think, didn't aim, didn't worry. She simply reacted—and pulled the trigger of her own gun.

CODY HAD MISCALCULATED GRAVELY. He'd gotten out of the truck and run, but the running made his vision worse to the point he started to question if he was even going in the right direction.

Everything was gray again, though he could make

out the difference between light and dark. Barely. He swore inwardly, standing God knew where, with absolutely no clue how to move forward.

Well, you have to. He reached out his hands, tried to find something to give him a clue as to where he'd run.

Then he heard voices and froze. Two men were talking as if they didn't have a care in the world.

"Always had to be a show-off," one man said, sounding vaguely amused. "I kinda hope they knock him around a little and we have to swoop in and save him."

"I wouldn't care if we didn't save him," the other man said. "I don't like dealing with kids." This one sounded gruff and irritated.

Cody could keep moving toward the sound, but he couldn't see well enough to move toward shapes or shadows anymore. He wouldn't know if they drew a gun or came charging. And worse, they would know he was having problems seeing and take advantage.

But he supposed as long as they were here, talking casually, they didn't know Nina had run across the yard a mile or so down the road. They didn't know if there was any trouble at the ranch. Maybe they figured their gunshot had scared off whoever.

"Ace can only do so much from behind those bars. He's going to have to name someone. We can't keep on like this. For all we know, that truck we shot out is going to the cops as we speak."

"If they're smart. We'll be gone by then though. Besides, what if Ace names this moron we're lackeying for?"

"A moron leader is better than no leader at all. Might get dumb orders, but no infighting."

"Boy, there's always infighting. Even under Ace."

Cody tried to determine where they were, based on voices alone, but when he didn't know where *he* was, it hardly mattered.

"You hear that?" one of the men asked.

Cody didn't have the first clue what to do, but he heard something too. An engine?

"We better move."

Then a gunshot pierced the air. Since Cody hadn't been expecting it, he jolted.

"We got company," one of the men said, and Cody knew he was screwed. Just. Screwed. He had to hope they didn't shoot him, or that if they did, he'd survive it. Surely they'd know he was Ace's son and not…

"That's one of Ace's, isn't it?" the more irritable man asked. "A Wyatt boy, aren't you?"

Cody hoped to God he was smirking in the right direction since he had a sense of where they were based on the sound of their voices. "I guess that depends."

"What's wrong with your head there, boy?"

They were getting closer, but they weren't shooting. Maybe Cody would have a chance to fight them off.

Two was going to be a lot harder than the one back at the Badlands, but he could do it. Surely he could do it if he had to, and with Nina off to save Brianna, he *had* to.

"Where'd he come from?" the one asked, and though he said it quietly, Cody still caught the words.

"Cat got your tongue?"

Cody wondered if the man had lifted a gun to point at him. There'd been menace in those words, a threat. Surely the threat was backed up with some kind of weapon.

So he held up his hands. "Not looking for any trouble, gentlemen."

One snorted.

"Better be careful screwing with a Wyatt until we know—"

"Would you shut up," the other man snapped.

"But see…why screw with one Wyatt boy, when you can screw with four?" a very welcome voice asked.

Cody couldn't see his brothers, but that was Gage's voice. Of course if they were here, where was—

"The house?" Cody demanded.

No one responded, and there was a bit of a tussle before Cody could hear Jamison reading the men their Miranda rights.

"You can't arrest us," one of the men argued, clearly still struggling to fight off Jamison. "We didn't do anything."

"I'm sure we'll find something," Gage said casually.

"One of them shot Felicity's truck." Cody didn't know which brother took him by the arm, but it didn't matter. "Brianna? Nina?"

"Everything was fine at the house when we left. We heard the gunshot and Brady backtracked just to make sure, but Tuck's back with Nina and Liza. I'm sure it's fine."

"I'm not," Cody returned. "Take me back to the house."

"Still can't see?"

"Comes and goes. Get me back."

Someone's phone chimed. "It's Liza," Jamison said, voice flat. "We all need to get back to the house."

Chapter Twenty-Two

The man was writhing on the ground, swearing and cursing at her.

Nina still held the gun trained on him, and Tucker had slipped in the opposite door and retrieved the gun the wounded man had dropped.

"Guess I shouldn't have insisted Sarah take my dogs to the Knight property." Dev looked down at the man with a sneer. "And just who do you think you are?"

"Wouldn't you like to know?" the man gritted out, holding on to his leg.

The shock started to wear off and Nina practically lurched for the ladder up to the hayloft. She could hear Tucker and Dev talking, but it was a kind of buzzing. She couldn't pay attention to the words. She had to get to her daughter.

She made it to the top of the ladder, scrambled onto the board of the hayloft and then looked around in heart-pounding panic. Where were they?

Then she heard the faintest sound, like a rustle. A whisper. She turned toward it, then moved toward it, right before a hay-covered tarp shook, moved, and two little heads stuck out from behind it.

Nina nearly sank to her knees, but instead she moved for them, grabbed them and held them to her. "Aren't you good, smart girls? You hid so good. You were so quiet. Oh, I'm so proud of you." She hugged them both, kissed their heads, tried and failed not to shed a few tears.

"There was a big noise, but I told Gigi we had to stay quiet," Brianna said solemnly.

"And we did!" Gigi said excitedly.

Both girls grinned, and it soothed something inside Nina. Terrible things could happen, these little girls could know they had to hide from bad men, but then they could stand up and be proud of themselves because they kept themselves safe.

They saved themselves, and maybe it wasn't fair they had to live in a world that made that happen—but wasn't it a miracle they could find some pride in it just the same?

"Uncle Dev saw the bad man and told us to hide. I knew just where to hide. Just like you always told me." Brianna snuggled into Nina's arms. "Where's Daddy? I pushed my button just like he told me."

Nina closed her eyes. Cody had known all along Brianna was the one who'd sounded the emergency alert. She couldn't work up anger over it. They were safe, and he was out there…

"We'll go find out." She stood, taking both their hands and helping them out from under the tarp and hay. "Come on now. Let's get you down."

"But where's Daddy?" Brianna demanded.

"We'll get him. Jamison and the boys are out getting him right now." *Please God.*

Nina helped the girls climb down the ladder, found Brady and Liza had joined Tucker and Dev standing over the increasingly weakening man bleeding on the barn floor.

"Come on, girls," Liza said, expertly positioning herself between their little gazes and the man's bleeding leg. "Cookies in the kitchen for being such good hiders."

Nina looked back at Tucker, Dev and Brady. "Where's—"

"I've called the ambulance to come pick up this one," Brady said, nodding toward the man. "I'll accompany him to the hospital. Jamison has the two guys you, er, ran into and is taking them to the jail. Gage has Cody and is bringing him back to the house."

"What about Felicity? We left her—"

"She already called. Everything is good there. She's got it handled. You go on with Brianna. We've got it here."

Nina nodded, grateful that someone had it. That it was over.

God. Please let it be over.

She trudged after Brianna, pain and exhaustion and the wearing-off adrenaline making every step feel like wading through lead.

Gage had Cody. Cody was safe. All the men who were part of this were being taken care of. For now, anyway.

She looked at her daughter bopping along with Gigi as though nothing horrible had happened. *For now* was okay. *For now* was better than okay.

CODY WAS SURPRISED at how long it seemed to take to drive back to the house, irritated that he had to be led into the ranch house, and then thrown into a world of pain when he felt two sets of arms squeeze around him.

He hissed out a breath, but bit back the groan of pain. "There's my girls."

And it felt good, even with the pain, to have them both back in his arms. Here in his grandmother's kitchen.

Everything would be okay. He *felt* that now.

"So, what on earth happened?" Liza demanded.

Everyone got situated around the kitchen table, and someone led him to a chair. Brianna climbed up into his lap and though he couldn't see her, he held her there, smelled her hair. She was fine. She was alive.

If he never regained his sight permanently, that was worth it right there.

"From what we figured out through the guys Jamison arrested, the man…" Cody stopped himself from saying *shot in the barn* in the nick of time. Brianna and Gigi didn't need to hear the full details even if they had to live through them. "The man in the barn was Andy Jay. Junior."

Gage swore under his breath.

"Obviously he blames the Wyatts for his father's death. It's not clear if Ace had twisted him to use him against us, or if he was using Ace to get to *us*. But either way, the lawyer was getting messages to Andy, who was leading parts of the Sons in Ace's absence."

"So… Nina shot the new head of the Sons?"

"Not exactly."

"Mom? You *shot* someone?"

He heard Nina's strangled response, which wasn't words so much as the sound a person makes when they don't know what to say.

"Brianna, can the adults have some time to talk by themselves? Is there something you and Gigi can go play?" Cody asked.

"I'll take them. Jamison can clue me in later," Liza said.

Brianna slid off his lap, and Cody knew he'd be having to talk to her about when it was appropriate to shoot someone, but first he needed to tell his brothers and Nina what they'd figured out.

Once he thought they were gone, Cody continued. "Andy Jay wasn't the new leader. They don't have a new leader. In fact, it sounds like the Sons are on shaky footing. I heard the two guys out front talking before they noticed me. The Sons are waiting for Ace to name a successor, and he hasn't. Infighting. Power vacuums. They're self-destructing."

"Well, then it's not a bad thing Andy Junior and his cohorts will be in jail for quite some time," Dev said gruffly.

"And with all three being taken care of, and Brianna occupied, I'm going to take Cody to the hospital," Nina announced.

"I don't—"

"You need a doctor," Grandma Pauline interrupted. "Let your woman take you to the hospital."

Your woman. He couldn't see, but he grinned in what he hoped was Nina's direction. "You going to take that label?"

"I'll take it," Nina replied, and her slim hand wrapped around his arm and tugged him back to his feet. "All the way to the hospital."

He grumbled, but he let her lead him outside.

"You don't have to do this, you know. I know I need a medical professional, but one of my brothers—"

"I'll take you. Because I love you." She stopped, brushed her mouth against his. "We're safe, Cody. And together."

"And we will be." He'd make sure of it.

Epilogue

It took a few days of rest, to the point he was going near crazy, but when he woke up a few days later his sight was back just as the doctor had predicted.

Not just the blurry in and out he'd had the first few days of healing, but full-fledged seeing.

His head injury had only needed to heal, and then his sight would too. And so it had. Thank God. He was really tired of being led around, even by the people he loved most in the world.

He sat up, looked around. Nina was curled beside him, clear as a picture underneath the big blue comforter. She was sound asleep.

Gorgeous. His.

Brianna bounded in, as was her current routine. She jumped right on the bed and grinned at him. "Can you see yet?"

"Looks like today's the day, B."

She gave a whoop of triumph, then launched herself at him.

Nina rolled over and yawned. "Now, you two. You still have to be careful. Healing takes time."

So much time. Time he was tired of. "You know, Jamison and I had a long talk last night."

"About bad guys?" Brianna asked, bouncing.

"No." He pulled Brianna onto his lap, slid his arm around Nina and brought her close. "See, Jamison and Liza and Gigi they all live in a town called Bonesteel. It's a short distance from here, not far. Liza's going to homeschool Gigi, and she thought your mommy could help her. So, you and Gigi would be in school together, taught by Aunt Liza and Mom."

Brianna's eyes got big as saucers. "I could go to school *with* Gigi?"

"And what will you do?" Nina asked, frowning up at him.

"Jamison said there's a computer repair store for sale. Owner would sell the building, the supplies, outright. I've got some tech skills."

"You're going to run a store?" Nina asked skeptically. "In Bonesteel?"

"A store. A front for some other things. Potato. Potahtoh."

She snorted out a laugh, and it was like in this very moment his world righted. Nina and Brianna were his. He had a plan for what he could do to help bring down the Sons—without being involved in North Star, though he planned to offer his services when they were needed.

And he could keep his family safe, because they *were* a family. "We could buy a little house. Have some slice of normalcy. Stability. Together."

Nina looked up at him, a considering look on her

face, so he gave Brianna the signal they'd practiced, tapping his nose three times.

She let out a little squeal, then scooted off the bed and ran out of the room.

"What are you up to?" Nina asked, skepticism still in place.

Cody dropped a kiss to the tip of her nose. He enjoyed the skepticism, Brianna's excitement, and as much as he didn't plan to do anything so sedate as run a computer repair business in a tiny town, he liked the idea of stability.

Of family.

Brianna scooted back in.

"You got it, B?"

Brianna nodded excitedly and jumped on the bed again. "Here, Mama." She shoved the box at Nina.

Who stared at it, eyes wide, much like Brianna had looked when he'd mentioned going to school with Gigi.

"Well, open it."

She flipped the lid, and there it was. The ring he'd bought all those years ago. Because Nina had always been right, and they'd already lost enough time.

"I love you. Both. With everything I am. We lost seven years. I don't want to lose a second more."

Nina looked up from the ring, tears swimming in her eyes. "I don't either."

"So. Marriage. House. Settle down in good old Bonesteel, South Dakota. Keep each other safe."

Nina reached up and cupped his face. "And happy," she said, as a tear slipped over.

"A family," Brianna shouted exuberantly, flinging her arms around both of them.

Because they were finally a family, just as they always would be from this moment forward.

* * * * *

*Look for the next book in
the Badlands Cops series
by Nicole Helm,
available May 2020
wherever Harlequin Intrigue
books and ebooks are sold.*

#1923 SECRET INVESTIGATION
Tactical Crime Division • by Elizabeth Heiter
When battle armor inexplicably fails and soldiers perish, the Tactical Crime Division springs into action. With the help of Petrov Armor CEO Leila Petrov, can undercover agent Davis Rogers discover secrets larger than anyone ever imagined?

#1924 CONARD COUNTY JUSTICE
Conard County: The Next Generation • by Rachel Lee
Major Daniel Duke will do whatever it takes to catch his brother's killer, but Deputy Cat Jansen is worried that he'll hinder her investigation. As the stakes increase, they must learn to work together to find the murderer. If they can't, they could pay with their lives...

#1925 WHAT SHE KNEW
Rushing Creek Crime Spree • by Barb Han
When a baby appears on navy SEAL Rylan Anderson's doorstep, he enlists old friend Amber Kent for help. But when the child is nearly abducted in Amber's care, they realize they must discover the truth behind the baby's identity in order to stop the people trying to kidnap her.

#1926 BACKCOUNTRY ESCAPE
A Badlands Cops Novel • by Nicole Helm
Felicity Harrison is being framed for murder. Family friend Gage Wyatt vows to keep her safe until they find the real culprit, but there's a killer out there who doesn't just want Felicity framed—but silenced for good.

#1927 THE HUNTING SEASON
by Janice Kay Johnson
After a string of murders connected to CPS social worker Lindsay Eagle's caseload is discovered, Detective Daniel Deperro is placed on protective detail. But Lindsay won't back down from the investigation, even as Daniel fears she's the next target. Will his twenty-four-hour protection enrage the killer further?

#1928 MURDER IN THE SHALLOWS
by Debbie Herbert
When a routine patrol sets Bailey Covington on the trail of a serial killer, the reclusive park ranger joins forces with sheriff's deputy Dylan Armstrong. Bailey can't forgive Dylan's family for betraying her, but they'll have to trust each other to find two missing women before a murderer strikes again.

HICNM0420

SPECIAL EXCERPT FROM

(H)HARLEQUIN

INTRIGUE

*Major Daniel Duke will do whatever it takes to catch his
brother's killer, but Deputy Cat Jansen is worried that
he'll hinder her investigation. As the stakes increase,
they must learn to work together to find the murderer.
If they can't, they could pay with their lives…*

Read on for a sneak preview of
Conard County Justice,
the next installment in New York Times *bestselling
author Rachel Lee's Conard County:
The Next Generation series.*

She wiped up stray crumbs, then tried to smile at him.
"Coffee?"

"I've intruded too much."

She put a hand on her hip. "I might have thought
so earlier, but I'm not feeling that way now. This is
important. I give a damn about Larry, and now I give a
damn about you. You might not want it, but I care. So
quiet down. Coffee? Or something else?"

"A beer if you have another."

As it happened, she did. "I buy this so rarely that
you're in luck."

"Then why did you buy it?"

"Larry," she answered simply.

For the first time, they shared a look of real
understanding. The sense of connection warmed her.

She hadn't expected to feel this way, not when it came to Duke. Maybe it helped to realize he wasn't just a monolith of anger and unswaying determination.

As Cat returned to her seat, she said, "You put me off initially."

Another half smile from him. "I never would have guessed."

A laugh escaped her, brief but genuine. "I'm usually better at concealing my reactions to people. But there you were, looking like a battering ram. You sure looked hard and angry. Nothing about you made me want to get into a tussle."

He looked at the beer bottle he held. "Most people don't want to tangle with me. I can understand your reaction. I came through that door loaded for bear. Too much time to think on the way here, maybe."

"You looked like walking death," she told him frankly. "An icy-cold fury. Worse, in my opinion, than a heated rage. Scary."

"Comes with the territory," he said after a moment, then took a swig of his beer.

She could probably wonder until the cows came home exactly what he meant by that. Maybe it was better not to know.

Don't miss
Conard County Justice *by Rachel Lee,*
available May 2020 wherever
Harlequin Intrigue books and ebooks are sold.

Harlequin.com

HIEXP0420

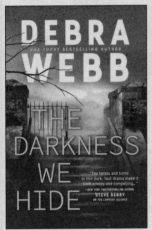

Love Harlequin romance?

DISCOVER.

Be the first to find out about promotions, news and exclusive content!

Facebook.com/HarlequinBooks

Twitter.com/HarlequinBooks

Instagram.com/HarlequinBooks

Pinterest.com/HarlequinBooks

ReaderService.com

EXPLORE.

Sign up for the Harlequin e-newsletter and download a free book from any series at **TryHarlequin.com**

CONNECT.

Join our Harlequin community to share your thoughts and connect with other romance readers!
Facebook.com/groups/HarlequinConnection

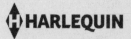